"Poor Rosemary," Frances said on her way to the kitchen. "It was a horrible thing to happen. Dreadful accident."

And as she left the room, Chetty spoke matter of factly from the front door: "It wasn't an accident."

Liam spun around. "How do you know it wasn't an accident?"

"Why should I tell you anything?" She stared at him fiercely.

"You don't have to," Liam agreed humbly. Their eyes locked.

Then Chetty's lower lip trembled. She sighed with relief at being able to tell him at last. "Well, O.K. then. I saw the car coming down the driveway—Mrs. Shapiro's driveway—we could all see it, and the big truck too. And I could feel it."

"*Feel* it? Feel what?" he asked the child gently.

"Just *feel* it. I don't know." Chetty faltered, confused. "It was kind of like something *strong* was there."

"And what happened after Mrs. Shapiro crashed into the truck?"

Chetty shrugged. "It went."

Liam sat quite still and looked at her. "Now listen very carefully, Chetty. Do you think—could it have been—I mean, that feeling—did it have anything to do with Mrs. Shapiro driving into the truck?"

"Sure," Chetty said, looking at him as though he were stupid. "It *made* her do it . . ."

The Neighbors

by Mary-Rose Hayes

PINNACLE BOOKS   LOS ANGELES

THE NEIGHBORS

Copyright © 1977 by Mary-Rose Hayes

All rights reserved, including the right to reproduce this book or portions thereof in any form.

An original Pinnacle Books edition, published for the first time anywhere.

ISBN: 0-523-40122-1

First printing, November 1977

Cover illustration by Ed Soyka

Printed in the United States of America

PINNACLE BOOKS, INC.
One Century Plaza
2029 Century Park East
Los Angeles, California 90067

For Patrick

Contents

THE NEIGHBORS

Prologue

Chetty watched Rosemary Shapiro die. She saw it all from the school bus; the municipal water district truck lumbering down the steep hill towards them, and the blue sports car tearing with lunatic speed from the Shapiro driveway. Gussy Ascoli, who drove the school bus and who possessed reflexes faster than he believed possible, wrenched the bus off the road, up the steep dusty shoulder, half grown with sun-scorched, spiky grass, his whole body flinching uncontrollably from the screaming of tires, the rending unmistakable sound of metal on metal, the heavy brutal crunch, the smell of overheated rubber and then the few seconds of terrible silence in which the only sound was that of liquid dripping slowly onto the ground. When the slewing truck came to rest, with the sports car crushed beneath it only yards from the front wheels of the bus, Gussy was able to back cautiously onto the pavement and park neatly, out of the way of the twin runnels of bright blood, gathering rounded bonnets of dust as they rolled downhill with growing speed, and the severed arm which lay apart, neatly sliced at the shoulder, still wearing a light blue cotton sleeve, at which the children gazed with silent fascination.

Gussy first took some seconds to vomit into a clump of purple ice plant, before throwing out highway flares and venturing closer to the crushed sports car and its mangled occupant. The dark green truck was canted across the street, already blocking three cars and a Chevrolet pickup on their way down, and within minutes, Gussy knew, there would be a sizable crowd. The truck driver, who was young with black hair worn long and a pair of bushy sideburns, leaned gray-faced against the door of the cab, his Adam's apple moving in his throat. Gussy rested a beefy arm across his shoulders. "It's O.K., man. I saw it. You couldn't've *done* nothing."

The truck driver gagged and sat down suddenly. Gussy searched inside the truck, found some old paper sacks, which he then arranged carefully over the arm. It seemed important to cover it decently and at once. And that was all he could do save wait for the police to come.

So Rosemary Shapiro, the gaunt-eyed woman who still mourned her four-years-dead husband, was dead too, now. In some ways, Rosemary's death could even be counted a blessing, for life had held no interest or pleasure for her beyond the contents of her liquor closet.

"It's not even as though she went to bars. Just bought all that booze and drank at home

2

alone," Gina Bombolini said. "By the case, too," Ardelle McNaughton added with disapproval.

"Poor thing," said Frances, for whom, as for everybody, Rosemary's death came as no real surprise. "Poor, pathetic thing. I suppose she's better off," her only emotion being mild curiosity as to why Rosemary was so urgent on the phone, so determined to speak with her. "Frances, I must see you. I have to talk with you . . . right now . . ." and overriding all Frances' excuses: "I'll come over to you. Now." And Rosemary had hung up on her, and now was dead, and Frances would never know what had been so important. Nothing, surely, that could have mattered; just some small trivia, suddenly overwhelmingly vital in Rosemary's sad, jumbled mind, to be told Frances at once. Why, she had barely even *known* Rosemary Shapiro, apart from an occasional meeting at a neighborhood gathering where Rosemary had been included out of kindness, and that one time she came up to the house, when she had said such crazy things. Oh dear, thought Frances, poor Rosemary. And now she's dead. I was the last person she ever spoke to, and I never knew her and never really wanted to. What a waste. She felt a twinge of shame that a friend—no, not a friend, just an acquaintance—had died and she barely cared. Frankly, did not care much at all. Her only feeling of outrage was for Chetty and the other children, that they should have to see something so disgusting, and she clung to that outrage because she felt so little these days, knowing by tomorrow it would have diffused

3

and merged into the bland apathy of the last three months.

The last day in Frances' life which had identity, whose events had shape and definition, was the first of July, now seeming so remote as to have happened many years ago to somebody else. July 1 was the last day she and Jack were just one other couple looking for a house in the suburbs.

It was the day they had found 40 Woodburn Lane. . .

CHAPTER ONE

July 1

Frances and Jack Driscoll passed under the swinging sign which said "Wilson and Steger, Realtors" in floral gothic script.

"We might as well look," Jack said. "Just for the hell of it."

And Frances shrugged, unenthusiastic. "I suppose. If you want."

In due course they were channeled to the desk of Wilbur Pfluger. He listened with devout attention to their needs, and told them with confidence that he had the perfect house—a brand-new listing, not even officially on the market until tomorrow—and they could see it right away . . .

"Well," said Wilbur, "what do you think? No, don't tell me. I can guess. This is it, right? Right."

"We'll think about it," Frances said sourly. Unlike Jack, she did not want to move from the city; she did not want a large suburban house, and she had carefully listed a great many conditions which all had to be met or she refused to move at any price, confident that the chances of finding all these features together were remote. But this house had everything. A complete upper floor, formal dining room, privacy, a beautiful view, big kitchen and low-maintenance garden. It was perfect. My dream house, thought Frances with exasperation.

"Think about it?" Wilbur's eyes widened. "But of course you must think about it." He gazed at them earnestly, a study of artless attention. "But take my advice and don't think about it too long. After all, how can you do any better than this? One acre on a prime lot? A panoramic view? Beautiful landscaping and old trees? And I'll bet the school bus right to the foot of the drive—you *do* have kids, right?"

"One," said Frances.

"School age?"

"Starting kindergarten in the fall."

"Wonderful." Wilbur looked very sincere. "A beautiful age. Now, can't you just see him playing in the—"

"Her," said Frances.

"A little girl. And the image of her dad, right?"

"No," said Frances. "She looks like me."

Wilbur bared his teeth in a strained smile. What was wrong with this woman? Anybody would think she didn't even *want* a house. Gripe, gripe. Dragging all the time. What a switch. Mr. Driscoll, now, was a real gentleman; no trouble at all selling *him*.

Jack said: "Fran, it's perfect. It has everything you wanted. Oh, come on, Fran."

6

The house was a gem by anybody's standards, and even the price was right. The owner must be nuts, decided Wilbur, for now things were loosening up; it was a seller's market. However, his was not to wonder why but to move the place as quickly as possible and pocket his commission, while marvelling that this was the first property in Woodburn Hills ever to come the way of Wilson and Steger. Properties in this neighborhood changed hands rarely and privately. It was so secluded here, so quietly, understatedly wealthy, a knoll and surrounding slopes, overlooking San Rafael in the valley below. At the highest point, commanding what must be one of the most spectacular views in the country, stood the Van Raalte mansion, in five wild acres of meadow and California wild oak; a huge, turreted Victorian, painted white, built in 1889 by Johan Van Raalte, the famed silver baron, as a country cottage for his eighteen-year-old English bride.

Johan Van Raalte's daughter still lived there. She saw nobody. She was very old . . .

"It's O.K. by me," Jack was saying. "How about it, honey? I mean, it's your decision. It's for you and Chetty."

Balls, thought Frances rudely. It's for your ego. But she said politely enough (she should not, after all, take out her resentment toward Jack on the unfortunate Mr. Pfluger, who was only doing his job) : "It's really a very nice house. But I just don't think people should rush into decisions like this. I mean, it *is* a lot of money."

True, Wilbur thought dismally, but tomorrow it will go on multiple listing. It'll be gone in half an hour. . .

But Jack said encouragingly: "Think how you'll be able to work here, Fran. So peaceful. And with Chetty in school every morning, with the school bus coming, like Mr. Pfluger said, so you won't have to be driving all the time—"

Frances paused, considering, thinking about peace and quiet, to which she was unaccustomed. Could Jack perhaps be right? Might she work well here? She might even be able to begin her novel, frustrated in San Francisco by continuous interruptions; *could* he have a point there, about peace? And despite the remote location, the freeway access was fast. She could be in the city in twenty-five minutes. (How negative, to buy a home for the speed with which she could leave it.) The privacy, another of her specifications, seemed absolute. Woodburn Hills was a mature neighborhood, certainly no tract—from downstairs she was unable to see even one other house. Only from one of the smaller bedrooms upstairs, through the gnarled branches of oak trees, could she see a portion of the next-door neighbor's roof. A tastefully rustic sign, she remembered, had announced discreetly: THE BOMBOLINIS.

"Well," said Frances. "Well, O.K. Maybe we'd better look around some more." And Wilbur Pfluger's anxious ear, honed over the years to a razor sensitivity, caught the first trace of weakening usually to be expected from a recalcitrant husband, and the tense strictures about his heart and throat relaxed with melting relief now that the commission on $92,500 might after all be his. "I'm telling you," he told Jack, "you folks are sure lucky, getting in ahead of everyone like this." And added: "If you asked me, I'd say it was meant. I'd say it was fate brought you into the office this morning."

That afternoon, Jack bid $85,000 for 40 Woodburn Lane. There was no counter-offer. "I can't believe it," he cried, jubilant. "Old Wilbur was right, that owner *is* nuts." And the house was theirs at the end of the month.

CHAPTER TWO

August 1

Chetty Driscoll was five years old, with curling blonde hair and thickly lashed green eyes. She did not like the house at all.

She demanded within five minutes: "Who'm I going to have to play with? Where are all those other kids?"

"What other kids?"

"All the kids you said I'd have to play with when we moved."

"They're around," Frances said comfortably. "We'll meet lots of people with kids. And school starts soon."

Jack said, surprised, "But she's right, you know. There aren't many kids around."

"Or *anybody*."

"Or dogs."

"Just that boy—" A lone teen-age boy, walking aimlessly down the street, who gazed after them from behind his thick glasses, his pale brown hair crew cut. "I didn't think any kids wore their hair like that any more," said Frances. "Not for *years*."

"I don't understand," said Jack. "I thought the suburbs would be crawling with little kids."

"I want to go home," Chetty said loudly. "I *hate* this house. And it smells bad."

"Smells bad?" Jack stared in astonishment, for the house had been scrubbed so thoroughly, and painted too. "Chetty, come on, that's *crazy*."

"No, I'm not, Daddy. It *stinks*, even."

"But darling," Frances said hurriedly, "don't you love your new room?" The first room to be redone, with gaily flowered wallpaper, white woodwork, a warm, shaggy orange rug and the new bunk beds which Frances had enameled white. "With bunk beds, you can have a friend to sleep over some nights."

"No," said Chetty. "I want to go home."

Liam Driscoll lay propped against cheerful, madras-covered pillows, absently scratching the contented rump of the marmalade tomcat on the rug with the toe of his sneaker, watching the gargantuan figure of Florence as she waddled back and forth to the bathroom with armfuls of dirty clothes. Many times he had offered to take her things to the launderette with his own; Florence always refused. She liked to wash her robes herself. She enjoyed plunging her thick hands into hot soapy water, and the scrubbing and wringing out of wet garments provided a satisfying physical counterbalance to the exhausting emotional drain of her afternoons.

Liam said again: "I can take all that stuff for you, Flo. Save your hands."

11

"Thanks," said Florence shortly, "some other time." As always she plodded about her daily tasks wearing orthopedic oxfords and a flowing muu-muu. Her muu-muus were all vivid, in stripes, flowers, or wildly flowing abstracts; today's had been wrought from a tie-dyed bed sheet and glared in radials of orange and purple. Florence possessed no outer or undergarments; once she had said vaguely: "Who cares? It's not as though I ever go out," and to Liam's certain knowledge, although callers and friends were too numerous to count, since he had lived with Florence she had never left the houseboat.

Once, in the early days, he had asked curiously: "Don't you ever want to go out?"

And she had stared at him as incredulously, Liam realized, as though he had asked her whether she wanted to go to Mars.

"Go out?" Florence had said. "Are you kidding? What for?"

Her mornings were spent in bed drinking cups of tea with her fifteen cats sprawling, a droning, furry quilt, across her lap and legs. After the tea, Florence dragged on her closest garment and waddled around her domain communing audibly with the dozens of plants which hung, swung, climbed and crawled or sat out on the deck in pots and planters. Then she would enter what she called her "comfortable" room, draw aside the curtain from her special closet and consider her robes. Her ultimate choice was a vital question, and one that would influence her bearing for the entire day. On white robe days she was glowing and spiritual; on pink days a loving earth mother; on green days she was matter-of-fact and brisk; on purple days reflective. With the onset of an occasional black day, Florence would demand that Liam hang the sign across the entry which read: DR. ROSSI IS NOT RECEIVING TODAY. On such days she would sit alone on one of the small folding chairs set in rows for the afternoon clients, who would arrive in anxious, possibly distressed clusters, bringing their urgencies and despair to lay upon Florence for the sum of one dollar. She would sit for hours, on those black days when she could not receive, when her power was neutralized by numbing, personal desperation, staring across the rows of ugly empty seats toward the table covered with the fringed Indian rug upon which stood a framed, tinted picture of two cherubim (one white, one black) and a vase of plastic lilies. Liam would leave, for he knew how overwhelming her burden could be.

It had been in just such a mood of sullen despair—"Oh, Jesus, please stop it—don't let me—Oh, God, why me? For Christ's sake, *why me?*" When he gazed unseeing into his beer in the No Name Bar on the Bridgeway in Sausalito—that he was taken to Florence. Three years ago, and he remembered nothing save that he had walked the two miles to Waldo Point through the darkness with a girl beside him who he seemed to have found, on some disconnected level of his brain, quite pretty. All he could remember of her was the glimpse of her old-fashioned buttoned boots in the headlights of passing traffic; he had walked wearily, his head lowered, feeling very old and quite exhausted. He had stumbled along lengths of rough planking, climbed some rickety steps into a warm, bright room filled with

13

stained glass, wind chimes, and luxuriant plants, where a monumentally fat woman played solitaire, using a deck of cards whose wicked, glowing faces were unknown yet at the same time wonderfully familiar to him.

The girl vanished; he never saw her again. Florence told Liam quite simply, above the contented vibrations of a dozen cats, "There's a bed through there behind the curtain. You'd better get some sleep."

"When you go out," Florence called from the bathroom, "I'll need some Tide and some other things. I'll give you a list. And you'd better take the money to the bank."

Liam listened to the splosh and thump of Florence's wash day, and to an off-key rendering of the "Habañera" from *Carmen*. Today, he guessed, would be a green day. Florence sounded very efficient. People would receive sound advice on money matters and business.

He swung himself lightly from his bed to help her carry her wash basket onto the deck, where she would peg out her robes on the line with old-fashioned clothespins. Unlike his older brother Jack, who at all times was filled with nervous energy and bounded as though on springs, every movement of Liam's was economical and calculated. "Lazy," said his father a thousand times, "plain, damn lazy," and his mother would bristle and turn on him, in defense of her baby, her afterthought, God's bonus, fifteen years after Jack, and him so certainly the last: "Lazy he's not; he just doesn't waste himself is all. Not like you at all, clumsy ox that you are."

And Chet Driscoll would retire with wounded mutterings. Liam was a thorn in his side, and a continuing source of bewilderment and irritation. Chet never knew how to approach him, what to say to him, how to begin to understand him, for Liam was so unlike his brothers, even in appearance. Sons to be proud of, the eldest three outstripped their small wiry father by more than six inches, grown tall and husky on good American food, on good meat, milk, and orange juice. All three were pale-skinned and dark-haired, with such grand navy blue eyes, lashed like a calf's. Irish eyes, Liam thought enviously, resentful of his own lean build and foxy freckled face. And the others had all become so successful; Pat the eldest was a priest, Kevin had his own construction company, and Jack was a partner with a firm of architects. Jack's world remained a closed and mysterious book to Chet, who had never struggled beyond the sixth grade, but he swelled with pride just the same for his third son was Somebody. Both Jack and Kevin were growing wealthy now, building up equity in houses, and *owning* things; they were accumulating stocks, savings and income property, while Pat, now Father Patrick Driscoll at the Church of our Lady of Perpetual Help only four blocks away, was presumably laying up his own spiritual rewards in heaven.

"And you, Liam," asked Chet, puzzled and hurt, "what's the matter with you? What is it you're waiting for? You can't be drifting about all your life."

A Friday family supper; a tradition, Frances hoped, that she and Jack could discontinue after their move across the Golden Gate Bridge, since it was after all such a long way to go every week with gas so expensive now. (An unconsidered plus for Woodburn Hills.) Present: The older Driscolls, Jack and Frances, Pat the Priest, Kevin with his wife, Marge, and Liam. Kevin saying: "You need a girl, Liam. There's nothing can't be fixed up by a good—" His mother saying: "I'll not be having that kind of talk at my table." Pat saying, worried: "It's three months now since you've heard the mass, Liam." His mother saying: "A good Catholic girl, now, Liam. Only yesterday I was talking with Mrs. Sullivan—you'll be remembering Kathy, now, Liam—such a grand girl." And all repeating, with the exception of Frances, at intervals throughout the meal, their own variation of the original theme. "What's the matter with you, Liam?" "You must do something, Liam." "Get a proper job, Liam." "Find a nice girl, Liam."

Liam Driscoll, nineteen years old in the days before Florence, possessing a gift which he hated. But, "It *is* a gift," Florence had said sternly. "It's a gift that you have; you're one of the very few chosen on earth."

Liam, very drunk, screaming: "Fuck you, you dumb, fat old woman. I didn't fucking ask for it. I don't want it. It's a curse, I'm telling you. It's a goddam, fucking curse. Do you hear me? I'll kill myself. I want to be dead. Leave me the shit alone."

Florence saying nothing, watching him, her mind for an instant touching his, guessing at the depth of his lonely despair.

"It's so lonely," Liam mumbled.

Florence sat on the bed beside him, which groaned and sagged under her weight. "I'll

16

help you," she said comfortably. "You'll learn to handle it."

Liam sobbed against her enormous, pendulous breasts. "But I can't. I don't know how. And I'm alone. There's nobody else—nobody else in the world."

Liam's loneliness ended when he met Florence.

And then, suddenly, he fell in love with Frances, although he was unsure of the exact moment when the emotional shift took place. For years Frances had been there in the background, fine boned and beautiful, built with the lines of a racing yacht, compared with Marge, a wide-beamed lobster boat. Amazingly, Frances had always been friendly toward him, and hers was the only uncensuring presence at the table during those dreadful dinners. But she had also just been Jack's wife, an adult, years older than himself. To Liam, at sixteen, twenty-seven-year-old Frances was immeasurably old. But at twenty, as though in a time machine, Liam felt the eleven years between them contracting, for Frances stayed essentially the same while he had matured both mentally and physically. And then there came the glorious day when he suddenly looked upon Frances with the same rapt, idealistic romanticism as a knight of old might have looked upon his lady; a thousand years earlier he would have galloped into battle with her token flying from his helmet. But, Frances being his brother's wife, and as such unapproachable and untouchable, must never, never guess (she did immediately), and he disciplined himself with a glorious, sacrificial restraint to limit his visits to once or twice a week, when he would

17

be casual and friendly so as not to raise the slightest suspicion. Liam would do anything for Frances. Nightly, from his solitary bed on the houseboat, he rescued her from blazing high-rises, car wrecks, sinking ocean liners, and muggers on the streets, to win her eternal gratitude and love, and no hint of eroticism crept in to disturb his romantic dreams for at least a year.

And then, shatteringly, right upon the heels of his love for Frances came his discovery of Chetty. One December afternoon, while Frances worked, they walked together in the park and played with Chetty's red and white striped ball, which was new and precious. Chetty was three years old.

It was an ordinary, homely afternoon. Liam had sat on a bench, watching Chetty pat a large, friendly looking dog of no recognizable breed. He closed his eyes momentarily against the thin wintry sunshine, and then cried out in shock as a barrage of frustration and anger ripped through his head, followed by Chetty's furious and very audible shouts. Liam found himself chasing the dog into the bushes, unaware of how he had got there, and wrestling the ball from its mouth.

"Doggie took my ball," Chetty said angrily.

"It's O.K.," said Liam. "Here it is. Better not let him have it; he'll just run off with it." And then, very carefully, he asked: "Chetty, what did you do just then?"

"When?"

"When the dog took your ball."

"I called you."

"I know," said Liam patiently, "but before

18

you called me, you did this——" and he showed her, very gently.

"Oh," said Chetty, shrugging. "Oh, that. Sure. It's easier that way. Isn't it?"

"Here," said Florence, "the money for the groceries, and we've finished the wine." She asked: "Did you hear from the kid yet today?"

Liam nodded. "She doesn't like the house," thinking with tolerance of the flashes in his head of wounded indignation, fired by Chetty with the disregard of bird shot. "She says it smells bad."

"So what?" asked Florence. "With some fusty old bat living there forty years, of course it smells bad. It'll be O.K. when they've cleaned it up properly and painted the place."

"No," Liam said cautiously, "Not like that. She says its a different kind of bad." He shrugged. "Not easy, when *she* doesn't know what she means."

"Anyway, if I can't see my friends, Uncle Liam will come over," pouted Chetty.

"Sure he'll be coming," said Frances, "but maybe not today. He was here yesterday. And we can't call him. Don't forget they don't have a phone."

"Of course they don't," said Chetty scornfully. "They don't need a——" and pushed her fist hurriedly into her mouth. "I don't think," Liam had said thoughtfully, "I don't think that we'll tell your mother and dad about how we talk to each other."

"Why not?" demanded Chetty, to whom it seemed so natural.

"They wouldn't understand. They're not like us. Let's just keep it our secret, O.K.?"

"O.K.," Chetty agreed, but sometimes it was hard to keep such a secret when one saw so much faster and clearer than other people.

"Chetwynd is remarkably mature for her age," wrote her nursery school teacher in the end-of-school-year report, "sometimes showing a most adult grasp of matters quite beyond her experience." She said to Frances: "I've never met a child like her before. Sometimes she even seems to know what I'm going to say before I've said it," and Frances nodded, understanding completely. "She's quite exceptional, you know," continued the teacher. "You'll have to be very careful with her—not push her on too fast, or frustrate and bore her. I'd say you were very privileged, Mrs. Driscoll."

"A genius," said Jack complacently, "graduating from college at sixteen."

"But she's *not* a genius," said Frances, puzzled, for in every accepted way of superiority Chetty seemed average, neither unusually gifted academically nor creatively brilliant. "She's just—different," frustratedly unable to envisage exactly how Chetty was different, but knowing her to be gauged by herself and by others on the wrong scale, and quite at a loss how to present this peculiar thought to Jack.

"Just—different," Frances repeated feebly.

CHAPTER THREE

September 1

During the month of August, Liam had found himself visiting the new house at 40 Woodburn Lane almost every other day. He never smelled anything bad. "Sort of a bit like the garbage," Chetty said, "when Mommy hasn't put it out for a while," although Chetty admitted that it was growing intermittent. "I just smell it sometimes, now. Uncle Liam, *don't* you smell it? Not ever?"

Liam shook his head. He asked Frances: "What did the termite report show? Any rot, or that kind of stuff that might do it? Did you check the drains?"

"No," said Frances, puzzled. "There's nothing. At least, nothing that could possibly be doing it. I think," she added, lowering her voice, "that whatever it is it'll get completely better as soon as she gets back in school."

"I suppose," said Liam. "You're probably right; she's bored," wondering what it was he himself found strange about the house, and suddenly realizing. Forty Woodburn Lane, although eighty years old, had no psychic vibration at all. No feel. It almost seemed suspicious in its innocence of atmosphere, like a long-time driver whose record showed not even one parking ticket. But maybe, Liam thought, it'll take me a while to become attuned.

He said: "It sure looks nice, though. You've done a terrific job. And so quickly."

Frances looked pleased. "And the floors look great, don't they? I can't tell you how glad I was to get rid of that tacky old wall-to-wall carpeting. Why do you suppose people cover lovely old oak floors?"

Frances, Jack, and Chetty, thought Liam, will probably plant their own vibes in this place. It doesn't feel like a *bad* house. It just doesn't feel so particularly great . . .

"And see this little rug," Frances was saying cheerfully. "We busted ourselves buying that. It was so gorgeous I absolutely had to have it."

"Yeah," said Liam obediently, "I like that," admiring the new rug, a small Bokhara in red and russet medallions which glowed richly against the polished floor.

Apart from this one new addition, the living room at Woodburn Lane was almost a replica of the living room in the old San Francisco apartment. The familiar pieces of furniture stood in roughly the same arrangement; the same pictures had regrouped over the fireplace, displayed against the same plain white walls, and the same two Persian rugs, larger but of lesser quality than the new Bokhara, lay underfoot. Nice, thought Liam, who sometimes craved continuity. Nice to carry your personal backdrop with you through life.

He said: "You were lucky, I guess, finding this house. Flo says you paid a good price for it, too."

"You know what we paid for it."

"Sure I do," said Liam, to whom $85,000 seemed all the money in the world. "But how'm I to know if that's *reasonable?* Flo understands money and all that stuff."

Frances said drily: "I guess she should."

"I wish you and Flo got on better together," Liam said wistfully. "Like you used to. She's a fantastic person, Fran. And you know how she loves to see Chetty."

"Yes," said Frances, "I know that. But she doesn't love seeing me. Not any more. It's hard, you know, to like somebody when they don't like you back."

Liam sighed, wishing the people he loved could at least tolerate each other, for Jack detested Florence and fumed at the countless times Chetty demanded to be taken to the houseboat. Jack's feelings, however, were mild compared with the outrage of his parents.

"I did not raise my son," thundered old Mr. Driscoll, "to live off a hooker on a barge."

"But she's not a hooker any more, Dad," Liam said sulkily. "She hasn't been a hooker in years. And you can't call it a barge, neither."

"Then will you be telling me where the money comes from," cried his father. "Will you be telling me *that*, then."

"Sure I can," said Liam in triumph, and rashly: "She's a clairvoyant."

"A— She's a what?"

"A clairvoyant. She has people in like, in the

23

afternoons, for readings, and they pay her, and she does, you know, faith healing. . ."

"Holy Mother of God," whispered Mrs. Driscoll.

". . . and she can read the cards, too," Liam added proudly.

Mrs. Driscoll broke into noisy sobs.

"Jesus, Ma—"

"You'll be saving your profanity for the outside of this house."

"Listen," said Liam in desperation. "She's a fat old woman. She has to be sixty-five years old. I mean, she's *old*. And she took me in, like, and I do a few jobs for her—"

"And will you be telling me what's wrong with your own home?"

"It's sinful," wailed his mother. "It's unnatural, a woman like *that* to live with a fine lad like you, and her not to—"

"Ma!" Liam broke in, shocked. "You don't understand. It's *nothing* like that. Nothing. How could it be?" And once again he mourned his total inability to reach his parents. His mother and father, and of course Pat, Kevin, and Jack, were quite beyond his reach. Absorption into someone else's mind, where one saw, touched, and actually *became*, for an instant, the other person, was a commitment so total and personal that with his family it imposed, to his own thinking, a kind of sexual taboo. Such contact would be almost incestuous, Liam felt with conviction, and unwittingly but successfully blocked access to them with his own inhibitions. With anybody else in the world, however—and for years Liam had walked the streets reluctantly and in fear, because the people would come to him instinctively, preda-

24

tory in their misery, to lay their burdens on his young shoulders—he would listen to the jumbled outpourings of poorly expressed and quite inadequate words while his mind reached uncontrollably into theirs, into gray places of confusion and fear, anxiety, hatred, and loneliness, for the images were the same and the identical burdens borne whether the sufferer be bank president, scholar, garbage man, wino, or priest.

His frightening gift placed a terrible strain upon him. He grew thin and haggard and was nearly always ill. Each winter his sore throats and coughing spells lasted for longer into the spring, and at eighteen years old he bought a fake I.D. and attempted to quench the nightmare in bouts of beer drinking.

It was the loneliness, most of all, which terrified Liam. It was not only inside him, but all about him, helpless and inarticulate. There was the memory of the old lady, which would be always fresh in his mind, no matter what Florence said, and the way she had stood beside him at the bus stop more than eight years ago, hands knotted in front of her, head bent to stare without hope at the filthy, gum-splattered sidewalk. She had mumbled: "I'm all alone. I don't have nobody. I'm sick. I don't have no money. I've nowhere to go. I'm going to kill myself, and I wanted someone to know. I just wanted to tell somebody, so somebody would know . . ."

"Oh no, oh, please," begged Liam, seeing a numb desperation so forlorn that he had turned and run away in blind panic.

"Maybe I could have helped her," he sobbed to Florence in an orgy of confession. "I could have done *something* for her, and I *ran away*."

"There was nothing you could have done," said Florence, adding with brutal practicality; "The poor old bitch was probably better off dead," and Liam gasped. "Oh, yes," said Florence, "I know just how that sounds, but I'm right, you know. She had no right laying all that on you—on a fourteen-year-old kid. No right at all. There wasn't anything you could do, and for Crissakes stop blaming yourself."

"But Flo—shouldn't I have tried, at least? I mean, shouldn't people try and help others?"

"Sure they should," Florence said with patience. "But like everything else, your first duty's to you. You have rights too. The way you were going, you'd have been burned out before you were thirty, or just plain driven nuts, and much good you'd have been to anybody then. No, Liam. Take care of yourself first, learn to pace yourself, and you'll still be around helping people out, if that's what you want, when you're ninety."

And now, at last, he was beginning to learn.

He was slowly able to shut off at will, no longer helplessly disseminating his own life-force into the atmosphere around him and drawing the misery of the world down upon him. He could look forward, now, to an adulthood free from the wracked desperation of his youth, to training this mysterious force inside him, which seemed to be his alone, into a concentrated, directed power, for use at his own will. It was as hard and demanding a training as for any worthwhile profession, and at times as discouraging, and forever in the future he would be delving into the farthermost reaches of his mind and discovering new wonders. "You'll never stop learning," said Florence. "Not until you die."

With a hopeful future ahead of him, Liam changed from the haunted, pathetically driven boy and filled out into a healthy young man. Florence bullied him, mothered him, and fed him home-cooked lasagna. Above all, she understood him, and under Florence's care, Liam blossomed. He discovered he had a sense of humor. He could laugh at last. And he noticed the world for the first time in its physical form. It miraculously began to grow a skin, a decent covering for the suffering beneath, and with shattering relief he knew he could be free from the terrible psychic currents which had battered him for so long.

He knew his mother imagined his present life to be one of unbelievable debauchery and excess, living with an aging prostitute who, even more outrageously, was not even a Catholic but practiced some outlandish religion and probably trafficked with the Devil. In reality, his life was so domestic as to be positively banal. "You have to have peace," said Florence. "Peace and protection, so you can grow." So he helped her with the housework, ran errands for her, fed her cats and occasionally collected the money at her afternoon sessions, depositing the takings three times weekly into the bank. Florence averaged $35.00 from her afternoons, and the cream came from the private readings in the evenings, at $20.00 for half an hour. It was enough for them to live on quite comfortably.

His thoughts turning from Florence, Liam asked: "Which of all these rooms are you using as an office? Did you start working again yet?"

Frances looked guilty. "Hey, not so fast. I can't do it all at once."

"But you should have fixed up your office *first*," Liam said disapprovingly. "You need to work, Fran. It's important for you. You have to be—" He groped for the right word. It was frustrating when with one mental stroke he could communicate exactly what he meant. Frances sat watching him, looking expectant. "You have to be—filled."

"Fulfilled?"

"Not quite. That comes afterwards. *Stretched* might be better."

"Oh." Frances felt again the familiar bafflement. He was twenty-two years old. She was thirty-three. Eleven years older. An experienced woman. What did he know about *anything*? And she knew he was right, as usual. (Chetty had once said: Liam knows everything.)

"Anyway," Frances said defensively, "this isn't so bad. I'm just taking a few weeks off to get things straight, and relax a bit after the move. Enjoy the peace. And you know what? The neighbors leave me alone here; it's great," admitting privately to a small feeling of pique (after all, it was more satisfying to have had the opportunity to seem superior), for the neighbors were either so unfriendly or so uninterested that nobody had bothered to come 'round at all. "Seen the neighbors yet?" Jack would ask hopefully, longing to be acknowledged by all the wealthy inhabitants of Woodburn Hills. "Not yet," Frances would reply with forced cheer. "Isn't it terrific, having all this privacy?"

"I'd love to meet that Van Raalte dame," Jack would say wistfully, "and the Bombolinis too. Isn't that a great name?"

"Probably Mafia," said Frances.

Liam asked: "Got any beer?"

"I'll get it," shrieked Chetty. "Let me get the beer," and rushed for the kitchen.

Frances unlatched the French doors of the living room, which opened onto a quiet patio, filled with camellias and azaleas. "Imagine it in the spring," Wilbur Pfluger had said. "All those blooms. Beautiful." "Come on," said Frances, "it's still hot. Let's sit outside."

Liam eased himself into a reclining seat, laced his hands behind his head, and squinted up at Frances with sheer pleasure. He never wore dark glasses, which she liked. "It's hard to talk properly with somebody if you can't see their eyes."

"Maybe that's Liam's secret," Jack said flippantly. "There's *never* been anyone who was talked to so much."

Happily drinking his beer in the sunshine, making desultory but comfortable conversation with Frances, Liam wondered how it would be, living Jack's life, everything nice and normal, with a wife and a little girl, and a house and a mortgage and two cars and an office to go to every day, and commuting and barbecues and insurance payments and car payments and regular meals and school buses and dinner parties and sometimes the Symphony and P.T.A. meetings and cocktails on the patio and nice clothes and ordinary friends and trips and . . . and . . . At times such as this he yearned jealously for Jack's life, for normality, for Frances to be *his* wife, for a child like Chetty. But that would never happen, could never happen to him, for he was different. He was an alien. Chetty was too, of course, but she would never know the desperation he had for he would always be there to help and guide her as, just in time, Florence had helped and guided him. "Electrical impulses," Florence had said matter-of-factly. "That's all it is: controlled vibration." But still, sometimes Chetty's vibrations reached him with such force he would be literally rocked back on his heels, his head bursting with pain. "*Never* send like that," Liam would cry in fury. "You have to learn control. Try again. More gently. Like this . . ."

"Sorry," Chetty would say cheerfully, and for a while her images would be muted. Only during intensely emotional moments was she still careless and explosive, but she was only five years old and consistent restraint came hard.

It was time to go. Liam finished his beer and rose to his feet.

"But you only just got here," Frances said, disappointed.

"It seems like that," said Liam, "but it's been a couple of hours."

"Stay and see Jack. He'll be back pretty soon."

"Some other time. Thanks for the beer, Fran."

"You never wait and see Jack. I wish you would. He misses you."

"Yeah; well I miss him too, Fran. I miss them all, really. But you know how it is—we start off O.K., for a few minutes, and then— Fran, I do *wish* I could talk to them. I really do."

Frances grimaced. "But he feels hurt when you come to see Chetty and me and don't wait to see him. Chetty always tells him you've been over—I don't want to ask her not to." She sighed. "But I know what you mean." She did indeed, for Liam and Jack were as unlike and incompatible as two brothers could be. Liam's very appearance underscored the difference, with his wild, rust-colored hair, heavy-lidded yellowish eyes and the queerly inverted tufted eyebrows which gave his face the look of permanent slight surprise. Against his dark and brawny brothers, the appearance of russet, narrow-nosed Liam was startling. "A cuckoo," Jack had said once, when Liam was still a child. "If Ma was a bird she'd have tossed you out on your fanny."

Frances found herself growing fonder of Liam with each passing week. Alone of his family, she admitted, she felt totally at ease with Liam, even more now than with Jack. *Much* more than with Jack. Why, she thought, with a sudden qualm, I could tell Liam anything. Just anything, and he'd understand.

But now she followed Chetty and her brother-in-law out to the driveway, where Florence's outlandish car, a 1953 Chrysler, cast a prehistoric shadow in the early evening sun. Liam kept its bristling areas of chrome glaringly polished; it was upholstered in fake wolf fur and painted in stripes in Florence colors— green, pink, white, and purple. Every six miles it consumed another gallon of gasoline, and Liam could not afford to drive it, at current gas prices, further than San Rafael to the north and San Francisco to the south. Woodburn Hills fell just within his northern boundary.

Jack despised the Chrysler, disparaged its poor mileage as thoroughly unpatriotic, and uneasily recognized his real feelings as embarrassment to be connected, even remotely, with someone who drove such an eccentric piece of junk. It was harmful to his carefully nurtured image, but Chetty adored the car. She found it so much more interesting than the prosaic, characterless Camaro and Volvo station wagon belonging to her own family. She and Liam spent happy afternoons together with chrome polish, rags and pails of water, Chetty laboriously and lovingly sponging the shark-like radiator grid, and very occasionally Liam would take her out for a ride, sitting speechless and small beside him on the enormous furry seat, tucked well back, legs stretched straight in front of her. "I wish you wouldn't," Jack said. "There's no seat belts in that old clunker. She could get killed." But Liam said, "I always go very slowly."

Frances and Chetty stood together in the lengthening shadows, and watched the barbaric striped end of the Chrysler as it disappeared down the driveway, feeling as always the small pang of loss whenever Liam left them.

"I do wish Uncle Liam lived with us," sighed Chetty.

Yes, thought Frances unwillingly, so do I.

"Hi, darling," Jack shouted boisterously. "How's Daddy's girl?"

"Fine."

"What did you do today?"

"I played; and I painted; and I found some roly-poly bugs—"

"Great."

"And guess *what*, Daddy?"

"What?"

"Uncle Liam came over."

"Again?"

"Oh, Daddy, you only just missed him."

Jack stood in the kitchen doorway, Chetty holding him firmly by the hand. "Fran? Liam was over again? That's an awful lot of visits—"

"Not really." Frances shook ice cubes into a bucket and began to slice a lemon. "It just seems like it is. Because nobody else comes here."

"Well, I wish he'd stayed. Couldn't you have asked him to stay over? He could have had dinner with us."

"He said he had things to do. He had to pick up something for Florence before the store closed."

"Errands for that goddam—" Jack released Chetty's hand. "Weren't you watching *Star Trek*? Go see what Dr. Spock's doing now."

"*Mister* Spock."

"O.K. *Mister* Spock. Go see him, because I have things to talk about with Mom."

They watched Chetty's back view, in blue and white Pooh Bear pajamas, as she headed, obediently, back to the television set. Frances poured Jack a drink. "What things do you have to talk to me about?"

Jack said nothing for a moment. He stared with utmost concentration into the brown gold depths of his Scotch and water. Then: "It's something I've been thinking about, on and off."

"Yes?"

Jack drew a deep breath and shook his shoulders. "Fran, it's Liam."

"Liam? What about Liam?"

"It's hard to say this," Jack said uncomfortably, "but it's been bothering me."

"What has?" asked Frances. "Or should I know something I don't? Has Liam done something bad?"

"I hope not," said Jack, "but now—well, hearing he's been over again—Oh, Christ, this is difficult, but I suppose now is as good a time as any. Listen, Fran. Something just seems wrong to me. I mean, he's always here when I'm at work; he never waits to see me. It's like he's avoiding me. Not that that's anything new—"

"But Jack—"

"Wait." Jack held up his hand. "Let me finish. You see, we never used to see much of Liam. The family, I mean. We don't have a lot in common. But these last couple of years he's around all the time. He's had a crush on *you,* you know, for years."

Frances shrugged deprecatingly.

"Oh yes, he has, Fran. Don't pretend you don't know. And I never paid any attention before, but he's not a romantic teen-ager any more. He's grown up. Fran, what do you and Liam talk about all the time?"

"*Talk* about? I don't *know* what we talk about. Anything."

"Well, I don't know how to put this any better," Jack said, ill at ease, busily swirling his ice cubes, meeting her eyes reluctantly. "But like I said, Liam's always been—I guess you'd just say 'different.' He doesn't think like other people. And he might do things—I wouldn't want to think that he was making any trouble for you, if you see what I—"

"No, Jack. No, I don't see what you mean. And anyway, it isn't just me he comes to see. It's just as much Chetty."

"Uh, uh. Not that Chetty's not a very cute little girl, but he wouldn't make a special trip to see *her*."

"I hope you're not leading up to what I think," said Frances coldly. "That's ridiculous. It's *sick*."

"Fran, it is not sick."

"But I'm almost old enough to be Liam's mother."

Jack laughed, and Frances went on:

"No, I mean it. To someone Liam's age, I'm old. I might as well be a *hundred* years old. No, Jack, you're being plain idiotic over this. Listen, Liam comes over to see us because Florence doesn't want him on the houseboat while she works in the afternoons, and he enjoys having a family situation he can relax in."

"But he already *has* a family."

"Oh, come on, Jack. You know better than that. You know how he feels about going home. No, he likes me, he feels comfortable here and he's quite fond of Chetty. That's all it is."

But Jack shook his head stubbornly. "I just can't buy that. Liam's an odd kid, but he's not so odd he wants to spend all of his time with an old woman like Florence, and a little girl of five. No, my sweet, it's as plain as plain. He's got the hots for you."

Oh, sweet Jesus, thought Frances, there are things that just should never get said . . .

"And if I didn't know him well, I'd even tell him to make sure he kept his cotton-picking hands to himself."

"But you don't *know* Liam," Frances cried indignantly. "None of you do. Not at *all.*"

"What the hell do you mean, I don't know my own brother?"

"No, Jack. No, you don't. And that's another reason he doesn't come around much when you're home. You make him feel uncomfortable. You're always picking on him, trying to make him something he isn't and can't ever be. He *is* different, Jack. You're right, but that doesn't make him some kind of freak. What's wrong with being different? Liam never hurt anyone in his life, so why can't you all accept him and leave him alone? Although," Frances said carefully, "I don't know Liam either; I doubt that anybody does except maybe Florence."

Jack sniffed. "I don't know what you're talking about. My brother Liam's always been a foxy kid who's never earned a penny of his own and never plans to, and hangs around my wife and kid a lot, sponging, when I'm not there. Of *course* I love my brother, but that doesn't mean I have to hand him you and Chetty on a platter. Christ, Fran, you must see more of Liam than you do me."

"You know," Frances said unhappily, "if Liam could hear you, or know what you're thinking of him, it would just horrify him. In some ways he's the—the most innocent person I know. He might have a few little fantasies, and I suppose he could have a crush on me, like you said, but as for actually doing anything *physical*, he'd rather die. I just know that. You know how young for his age he is, that way. I mean, I don't think he's ever had a girl friend, even."

Jack shook his head. "Of course he has. He must have."

Frances sighed.

"He's twenty-two years old, Fran. Probably just ashamed of Ma and Dad. Never brought his dates home."

"Liam would never be ashamed of anything," said Frances.

And Jack, suspecting belatedly that he had gone too far and pushed too hard, said with attempted lightness: "Liam's so pure, maybe it's him should have been the priest in the family instead of Pat."

The strained meal was over, Chetty long in bed, and Jack and Frances sat in the sun porch, looking out over their garden, the oak trees, the lights of San Rafael and finally the endless, brilliantly unwinding snake of Highway 101. They had not discussed Liam over dinner, but he was there, an unseen third presence at their dinner table.

Jack said, determinedly cheerful: "You know, I think this is all pretty much perfect."

Frances said, startled: "Perfect?"

"I mean, this house, and the life out here. You are happy here, aren't you, Fran?"

"Are you asking me, or telling me?"

"Just promise me, Fran, that you'll give it a chance." Jack looked at her anxiously across the top of his wineglass. "My God, most people I know would give their right arms to own this house. You simply can't beat it. Just look at that view. Look at it, will you? And the terrific garden, and the trees—"

"And the school bus right to the foot of the driveway—"

"And really, Fran, it doesn't take me much longer to get to the office than it did in the city. I've been thinking I might take the ferry, sometimes, you know. From Sausalito."

"That would take much longer."

"I know, but think how refreshing, to start and finish the working day with a boat ride. You have to look at the total way of life."

"Oh all right," said Frances. "I'll buy that. Pour me some more wine, and we'll drink to the American Dream."

From their bed they gazed through the opened glass doors into the tops of the trees, above which, tonight, hung a huge bronze moon.

"Hunter's moon," murmured Jack.

"No, Harvest moon," said Frances. "Hunting comes later."

"Wrong," said Jack. "Hunting now." His hand slid between her thighs and he drew her toward him, dismissing her passivity, rejecting the reason for it. He drew her on with him for a long time, determined to win her, and beneath him, coolly watching the moon over his bent head, she thought how beautiful the gleaming outline of his arched shoulders, the dip of his spine, his tensely supporting arms, herself standing somewhere apart, witness to her own body's automatic responses, for the first time essentially unmoved but aware of her continuing body hunger and of how Jack was still one of the few to ever satisfy it.

They lay together, intertwined, warm and sated.

"Love me?" said Jack.

"Yes," said Frances, from her cool, far place. "Yes, of course."

CHAPTER FOUR

September 4

Evangelina Bombolini said: "What *could* we have done about it? There was nothing—"

Eleanor Spriggs said: "Just taking off like that, without telling us."

Joanie Spritzer said: "Dying in Kansas *City,* yet."

Barbara Woods said: "And we didn't *know.* A real mess, if you ask me."

Ardelle McNaughton said: "Nobody was."

Rosemary Shapiro said nothing.

The six women stood aimlessly in the living room of the Van Raalte house. They awaited the entry of Helena Van Raalte before sitting down and daring to drink the coffee waiting in the Wedgwood coffee pot, surrounded by small porcelain cups and saucers, and the silver cream pitcher and matching sugar bowl for the brown crystalline sugar Mrs. Van Raalte ordered specially from Fortnum and Mason in London. The aroma from the coffee was tantalizing. Barbara Woods whispered to Gina Bombolini: "She always does this. Makes us wait. I can't stand it . . ."

The room was large and airy, with picture windows overlooking the valley. The walls were painted pale green with molding picked out in white; the carpet was the color of deep, soft moss. The furniture was antique, glowing with care and arranged with taste. Against such rich and elegant surroundings, the six women grouped awkwardly around the coffee table looked glaringly out of place. "A tacky group," Mrs. Van Raalte had sighed more than once. "No class. None at all. But one has to make do with the tools available, I suppose . . ."

There was Evangelina Bombolini, of them all perhaps the only one in whom Mrs. Van Raalte could be said to confide, however remotely. Gina Bombolini dominated the group by sheer size. She was grotesquely overweight, her flesh the color and texture of lumpy dough, wearing an unbecoming yellow house dress which fastened precariously across her bulging breasts. Eleanor Spriggs was tall and desiccated, dry brown skin eroded by years of unheeding exposure to harsh weather. She stood aloof and silent, eyes watchful under drooping saurian lids. Eleanor spoke seldom; when she did, people listened. Joanie Spritzer, unmistakably over forty, wore the top three buttons of her blouse roguishly unbuttoned, a suede miniskirt and six-inch purple platform shoes. Barbara Woods and Ardelle McNaughton, next-door neighbors who hated each other, seemed interchangeable in the successful young suburban matron uniform of tailored polyester knits and bubbly hair styles. Rosemary

Shapiro lit a third cigarette with hands that trembled, wondering in desperation how long before she could escape, close her own front door thankfully behind her, and lose herself to the anguished relief of her liquor closet.

"You were saying, Barbara?" Mrs. Van Raalte asked from the doorway. They all turned, flustered. She was always so silent, so quick. She stood watching them, smiling with her heavily painted mouth, the thick mask-like makeup on her cross-hatched face already splitting and flaking. But the fine black eyes still glowed, deep-set and unflawed from beneath lids which sagged under their heavy burden of blue eye shadow and beaded black mascara.

Barbara flinched.

"Sit down, won't you," Mrs. Van Raalte said graciously. "And please help yourselves to coffee."

She seated herself in a huge, Victorian winged chair, her childishly small feet in the black-button shoes and gray silk stockings set primly together, barely reaching the floor. She said: "Gina, perhaps you would be kind enough to pour. I shall take mine black as usual."

There was a flurry with the tray, with cream and sugar and spoons. Mrs. Van Raalte sipped her coffee, waiting.

Eventually she coughed, gently. There was instant silence.

"Well now," said Mrs. Van Raalte, "I'm quite sure you all know why we're here. We have a problem, don't we. Oh, dear me, yes."

She listened, amused, to the chorus of anxious cries. She replaced her cup on the tray, its rim now adorned with a greasy, magenta half moon, and continued: "How did this disastrous situation come about in the first place? Am I not able to turn my back for one minute?"

"But, I never thought—"

"I mean, we all knew she was getting a bit senile—"

"And you were away and we didn't want to disturb—"

"*I* never knew anything about it."

"But who would have thought she'd have been so stupid? It's not as though she was—"

"Oh, be quiet," sighed Mrs. Van Raalte. "All of you." There was another immediate silence, marred by Rosemary Shapiro whose shaking hand rattled her coffee cup in its saucer. Mrs. Van Raalte ignored her. "So Mrs. Demetrios decides to visit her daughter in Kansas City the week after I leave for Europe. And the fool dies there." She sniffed disapprovingly as though regarding the act of dying to be in questionable taste, gazing round the circle of strained, expectant faces, thoughtfully holding for a few tense seconds the haunted eyes of Rosemary Shapiro. "Not that she was at all suitable for our project in the first place." She told Ardelle McNaughton: "Alan is old enough now to replace Mrs. Demetrios. He may do so at once. And with regard to his—uh—aberration, you will see to it that there are no incidents. It will not do to attract attention."

Ardelle shifted in her seat. She whispered: "Yes. I'll talk to Alan."

"But now?" Gina Bombolini's jowls quivered in worry. "What are we to do now?"

"And of course," Mrs. Van Raalte said, ignoring the interruption, "no one thought fit to

43

inform me of this idiot Demetrios until it was too late."

"But we didn't even know she was dead."

"Until the movers came for her stuff—"

"And the house was sold already. It went just like that; so fast you wouldn't believe."

"There wasn't even a 'For Sale' sign up, not for a day."

"And so," continued Mrs. Van Raalte, "before I could make suitable arrangements for the disposal of the property, and *before I was even informed*—" She turned a hard stare on each individual in turn, whose faces froze like terrified rabbits, "living right here, so to speak on the doorstep, we have the young Driscolls."

There was a short, agonized pause.

"I thought," Mrs. Van Raalte continued, laying a stapled sheaf of papers on the coffee table, "it seemed useful to know something about the Driscolls. It was easy enough . . ." She fumbled for the black-rimmed bifocals which swung from her neck on a thin cord, and picking up the topmost paper, the first in a three-page report from the O'Hare and Brundage Agency, she began to paraphrase.

"Jack and Frances Driscoll are thirty-seven and thirty-three years old respectively, formerly residing at 4049 Jackson Street, San Francisco. Jack Driscoll is a partner of Koenig, Thomas and Driscoll, Architects: Frances Driscoll is a free-lance writer, contributing to the *San Francisco Examiner* among other publications. Jack Driscoll has three brothers, in order of age: Father Patrick Driscoll, forty-two; Kevin, thirty-nine, and Liam, twenty-two. Kevin has a small construction company; Liam is unemployed and lives on a houseboat in

Sausalito. Jack Driscoll does not appear to have a close relationship with any of his brothers, with the possible exception of Liam, who was once observed to visit the house during the three-day period of surveillance. However, Liam does not appear to be the kind of person to pose any problems to us. The parents live in the Mission District of San Francisco on Valencia Street. Mr. Driscoll is a retired dock-worker.

"A profile on Jack Driscoll shows him to be a moderate social drinker—" Mrs. Van Raalte's eyes again fastened derisively on Rosemary Shapiro— "and he does not associate with women other than his wife. He drives a 1975 Camaro; his driving license is clean. He plays tennis at the Golden Gateway Center approximately once a week and vacations during the summer with his family at Lake Tahoe. His assets are reasonable and his debts unremarkable. Naturally he is a Catholic, but does not attend church regularly. In other words," Mrs. Van Raalte said cuttingly, "Jack Driscoll is your stereotyped upwardly mobile middle-class bore."

"I don't understand," said Gina Bombolini. "Why go to all this trouble? Couldn't we just—"

Mrs. Van Raalte raised heavy black eyebrows. Gina quailed and fell silent, and the old lady continued. Her voice sharpened. "However, Frances Driscoll may be more interesting. She comes from New York City; she majored in journalism at Columbia University; she has no relatives in the San Francisco Bay area and has little contact with her husband's family. Her mother lives in Boston,

Massachusetts. No problem there. Frances is socially active; belonging to various organizations including the Museum of Art Auxiliary, the San Francisco Ballet Association and a professional women writer's group. She regularly attends art gallery functions, and is known to have a wide circle of somewhat avant-garde friends."

Mrs. Van Raalte ran her large, pale tongue over her lips and said: "Possibilities here, wouldn't you say? Naturally I could not authorize an investigation into her more personal habits without arousing attention."

The other women looked bewildered.

Mrs. Van Raalte leaned forward, clasping her knees, and rocked slightly back and forth, her eyes gazing unseeing at the hazy wooded hills across the valley. Her pulpy mouth opened, her tongue flicked at her red-stained teeth. She said softly, and every woman in the room attuned with hushed expectancy: "So we must find out for ourselves. We will become very friendly with Frances Driscoll. She has moved here recently from the City, she will be lonely, and she will be vulnerable. There will be no family, friendly pastor, or familiar faces at the grocery store." With a grotesque parody of concern, she added: "You must all be *very* nice to Frances. Become real friends. Get to know her well. Win her confidence, and see what comes up. I am particularly interested in her sexual tastes and proclivities, and any possible past indiscretions. You might start with general gossip, past men in her life, maybe? I leave it to you." Again her gaze swept the room, somber with restrained excitement.

46

"You are naturally wondering whether I, myself, have gone crazy. I can see the thoughts in your heads." Mrs. Van Raalte permitted herself a chilly smile.

Rosemary Shapiro shuddered.

"But when I tell you one more fact, then things will become clearer. As to the rest, you will learn all in good time. You see, the Driscolls can be quite valuable to us. Their arrival in our midst is, in fact, timely. They can save us a great deal of trouble, oh yes indeed." The woman leaned forward, confused but with interest firmly aroused, and Mrs. Van Raalte, pleased to hold them in suspense, to have saved this extra morsel for the last, told them: "The young Driscoll's have a child. Allison Chetwynd. She is five years old. Think about it."

SEPTEMBER 6

"Guess what? I met one of our neighbors today," said Frances.

"About time. Which one? The Black Widow?"

"No. Gina Bombolini."

"Aha. So tell. What's she like? Gorgeous and Latin-looking?"

"Well—she's Latin-looking. With a big moustache. And very fat."

"Jesus!"

"She's really very nice," said Frances. "She

said they'd been on vacation, or she'd have stopped by before."

"Fair enough."

"Only thing," Frances said, frowning. "I've seen cars in their driveway, and I'm sure I saw her driving by on the street last week."

"So what?" said Jack. "Maybe she wanted an excuse so's not to hurt your feelings, or maybe they really were away and had house sitters. What does it matter?"

"You're right," said Frances. "It doesn't matter. But listen to the good news: they have a sixteen-year-old daughter, Constancia, yet, who's a junior at San Rafael High. A built-in baby sitter. Gina says she doesn't go out much—have many dates or anything."

"If she looks anything like her mother, I'm not surprised."

"Gina says she prefers to stay at home. Apparently she's a brain, straight A's in Math, Physics, and all that stuff. And she'd love to baby-sit. Let's have her tomorrow and try her out; I hope Chetty likes her."

Chetty said unexpectedly from the doorway: "Who'm I supposed to like?"

"Connie Bombolini. She's going to baby-sit for you."

"Connie Bombolini? Yecch," said Chetty.

Connie Bombolini, almost as fat as her mother, was already breathing heavily by the time she had walked up the driveway.

She's *awful*, Frances thought guiltily. Chetty thought so too, demanding of Frances: "Must I have her? She's gross." And of Connie, mercilessly: "Have you got a baby in your tummy?"

48

"It's not just that she's so fat," Frances said in the car. "She's got a repellent personality. Oh, poor Chetty. I hate to leave her with somebody like that."

Jack laughed. "If they're pretty and on a diet and lots of fun they have dates all the time. You can't win."

"I suppose," said Frances. "I know I'm being unfair."

"Anyway, Chetty will be in bed in half an hour. It's not as though she'll spend any time with Connie. Relax. You don't have to have her in the daytime."

"During the day? Good grief," said Frances, "are you kidding?"

SEPTEMBER 8

A day of brassy September heat; the air hung heavy and saffron below in the valley. Frances sat in a redwood recliner beside the Bombolini pool, sipping from a glass of iced tea in which the ice was already melted, wondering how soon she could leave without appearing rude.

Of the six women invited to the Bombolini house for mid-morning refreshments, only Rosemary Shapiro appeared impervious to the heat. She gratefully drank straight vodka over ice, and the morning trembling of her ill-kept hands was steadying. Her eyes, too, were calmer, staring at Frances from their umber sockets with something approaching intelligence. It was hard to guess her age. Perhaps

49

forty-five? wondered Frances, realizing with a small shock that Rosemary must have been pretty when she was younger.

"Hot enough for you?" asked Joanie Spritzer.

"It sure is," said Frances. "It doesn't usually get this hot in the city."

Gina Bombolini, puce-faced and sweating, said: "Anyhoo, I hope you'll be real happy up here, Fran. Can I call you Fran?" Be nice to her. Be real nice to her. Invite her to your homes. Find out what makes her tick. And report.

"Sure," said Frances.

"Tell me," said somebody (tall, with skin like a lizard—outdoorsy looking. Eleanor something? Must be.) "What work does your husband do, Fran?"

"He's an architect, Eleanor."

"And how is he finding the commute?" Barbara or Ardelle; difficult this one. Both in bermudas and fussy tops, lacquered hair-hats still bravely staunch against the wilting heat.

"He doesn't mind (certainly he didn't; it was a status symbol, being a commuter. Jack managed to bring it into almost every conversation). He comes home just a half hour or so after the rush hour, and he says it really doesn't make much difference. The traffic's much better by then."

"And how do you like it? Living in Marin?"

"It's a change," Frances said cautiously.

Rosemary Shapiro rose without a word, heading stiffly for the wet bar like a robot on a homing beam. "That's right, dear," Gina said comfortably, "just you go make yourself at home." She fanned herself vigorously with a paper napkin, mopped at her streaming face and surreptitiously opened her legs wider on the recliner. In the heat and with her bulk the insides of her thighs sweated and chafed together unbearably and now had the consistency of raw meat. She half rose to shift her position, groaned involuntarily, and said: "You have such an adorable little girl. Connie just loved baby-sitting. She never gets the chance to baby-sit—there just aren't any little kids up here. She loves little kids."

"That's great," said Frances. "We used to have a hard time finding sitters in the city. Mostly families move out when the kids get old enough to be of any use." She turned to Ardelle McNaughton, who sat on her left, asking politely, "Don't you have a son?"

Ardelle nodded. "He's seventeen."

"Is he quite tall? With brown hair and wears glasses?"

"That's him. That's Alan."

"We saw him when we first came up here, out walking."

"He likes to walk."

"I guess he'll be going to college soon, Ardelle? Does he have any particular interests? For a career, I mean?"

Barbara Woods said: "He's real fond of animals. Especially dogs. A veterinarian, maybe?"

"Why, good morning, officer, has there been an ac—"

"This your boy, ma'am?"

"Yes—yes, of course. That's Alan—"

"Don't listen, Mom, what they're going to say. I didn't do it, Mom. It wasn't me. It's a mistake, Mom."

51

"I'm real sorry, ma'am, having to tell you this, but—"

"Alan's never been in trouble, officer. I'm sure there's some mistake—"

"Not this time, ma'am."

"You leave Alan alone, you hear?" snapped Ardelle, flushed and angry.

"Alan a vet," smiled Barbara nastily. "That's good. That's real good."

The future career of Alan McNaughton appeared a sensitive topic, and Frances was relieved when the conversation swung to more general matters.

"Do so hope you'll be happy up here."

"Where are you sending your little girl to school?"

"Just the best schools in San Rafael."

"So private up here."

"A really nice bunch of people; almost like a club."

Frances glanced about her at the other women, not at all anxious to be included in their "club." She sipped her tea, and said, "You know, what I would really like is to meet Mrs. Van Raalte. I've heard so much about her."

The moment of complete silence was startling. Then Gina said abruptly, "What have you heard?"

The tension was palpable, as though Mrs. Van Raalte could make her presence felt all the way from the hidden mansion on the knoll. Frances said, disconcerted, "Oh, nothing much. Only ordinary things; gossip from realtors and stuff that's all. And the Fuller Brush Man. She just sounded like a—quite a character. That's all."

Rosemary Shapiro, well into her fourth drink, spoke for the first time. She said with bitterness: "She's a real character all right. And a real —"

Gina said quickly, in a high-pitched voice edged with panic: "You shut your mouth, you hear?"

And then they all looked nervously toward the hill top. Frances, helplessly nonplussed, stared at each tense face in turn.

Rosemary staggered to her feet, knocking over her glass of frosted plastic, which bounced unharmed toward the pool edge, scattering the remains of ice cubes and a sliver of lime. Joanie said: "You'd better go lie down, honey."

Rosemary nodded. "It's the heat . . ." holding her hand to her mouth as though about to vomit. "I guess it's the heat." She lurched clumsily into the house without saying good-bye to anybody, catching her shoulder on the edge of the screen door.

Eleanor Spriggs sighed. "Poor Rosemary."

Joanie said, "Ever since Don passed away."

No allusion was made to Gina's strange outburst, and everyone now spoke at once to gloss over the awkward moment. To Frances' disappointment, Mrs. Van Raalte was not mentioned again.

"It's a good day for a swim," said Joanie. "We should've all brought our suits."

"It must be way over ninety."

"And so dry."

"Did you read about the forest fires up north?"

"Only a month or so until the rain starts."

"I can't wait."

"The yard never seems to get enough water."

What would they be talking about, suddenly wondered Frances, *if I wasn't here?* She said: "I hope Rosemary is all right. Shouldn't somebody check?"

"Sure she's all right," said Gina. "She shouldn't drink that way in this heat. Not and expect to stay on her feet."

"I guess not," said Frances.

"I hear you're a writer?" said Joanie.

"Well, yes. Trying."

"How exciting. What do you write? Would we have read anything you wrote?"

"I don't know," said Frances. "Unless you read the magázine section in the Sunday papers. I sometimes have pieces in there. Maybe you read my article last year on dog sh— on the city's pet problem. It got a lot of publicity." She had been proud of that article. It was amusing, and tautly written. "One watches one's step on city sidewalks." she had begun crisply, "as though negotiating a minefield," and had continued with various horrific stories of pet overpopulation and the by-products thereof, including the incident of the skate-boarding teen-ager who had hit just such an obstacle, been thrown, and broken his arm.

Never before had this failed to raise at least one shocked giggle, but now it appeared she had quite lost the attention of her audience.

"So I guess I'm just not too crazy about dogs," Frances said lamely, after her story had fallen flat. "Jack wants to get one for Chetty. Guess who'll get stuck with taking care of it?"

"Oh yes," Gina said vacantly. "It happens all the time."

After Frances had left to meet Chetty at the school bus stop, Gina said: "So, where does that get us?"

"Nowhere much."

"Who *cares* what she thinks about dogs?"

"If she'd written sexy stuff, maybe—"

"But *why* are we supposed to find out about her sex life? What does that have to do with anything?"

Gina looked grim. "There's always a reason."

A pause.

"And I guess we have to start somewhere," Joanie said.

"Sure," said Ardelle. "We'll take it on from here. I'll have another Tupperware party next week and ask her over."

"Make it in the morning," said Gina. "Fix lunch afterward. Give her some cocktails first."

Joanie said: "I'll have them over for dinner. That husband's a cute-looking guy."

"O.K.," said Gina, "but watch it."

Joanie looked sulky.

"And Ardelle—you just better remember about Alan."

Ardelle sighed. "I'm trying, but it's a long time for him to wait. I mean, him being so young, he doesn't even think like us. Dying doesn't have any meaning for him." Then: "I'll fix him," said Ardelle hurriedly. "I really will. I promise."

"Do that," said Gina, adding: "And we'll all have to watch out for Rosemary. You girls will understand. We can't *trust* Rosemary any more, these days. She and Frances shouldn't get together alone."

They nodded slowly in unison, and Gina sighed, thinking of them all, in particular of Rosemary. There was so much at stake. Had that stupid fool said too much? And this new aspect of the affair, this whim of Mrs. Van Raalte's to involve the Driscolls. Gina Bombolini's whole being rebelled although she would never dare to say so. We would have managed, thought Gina, the way we had planned it. We don't *need* the Driscolls. But now they were here, to be dealt with advantageously, to be stage-managed invisibly by Mrs. Van Raalte. Madness, thought Gina resentfully.

But in the meantime, something had to be done about Rosemary, and *she* had to be told the outcome of the morning's session. Grunting in pain, Gina heaved her moist bulk from its supine position on the chaise, and walked carefully inside, feet widely spaced, to telephone.

SEPTEMBER 12

"It's somebody called Ardelle McNaughton," Jack said. "For you."

"Hi, Ardelle," Frances said into the phone. "How are you today?"

Jack returned to his weekend task of hanging Frances' spice racks in the kitchen, smiling happily. The neighbors were coming through at last. It had taken a while, but they seemed to be a friendly group after all, which would be

56

nice for Fran, for he knew with a twinge of guilt that she felt a bit cut off up here. And as for his unspoken dread that the Driscolls would not prove socially acceptable in Woodburn Hills, why, that had proved to be nonsense.

"Ardelle, that's really nice of you," he heard Frances say, "but I'm busy, I'm afraid. I have a doctor's appointment in the city. But thanks for asking me, though. Could I take a rain check?"

She pranced into the kitchen, grinning, to tell Jack: "You won't believe it. I've been asked to my first Tupperware party. Where have I been all these years?"

"You aren't going?"

"Are you *kidding*?"

"Well—you might meet some more of the neighbors. It might be fun," said Jack seriously.

"Well, forget it," said Frances. "I think I'd rather do almost anything than go to a Tupperware party."

"All right, *all right*," Jack said. "It's not that big a deal."

"Tupperware party," said Frances. "Good grief. As though I didn't have a million other things—"

"She was only trying to be nice," Jack said mildly. He carefully marked the screw holes for the rack with a pencil. "D'you think that's level?"

"Yeah," said Frances. "No. The right end is a little bit lower than the left."

"It *has* to be straight. I used the spirit level."

57

"It doesn't look straight, though. The wall's most likely off a bit."

Jack ignored her and drilled two holes for the supporting hooks. Frances said: "Do you think I *ought* to go?"

"Go where?"

"To the Tupperware party. At Ardelle McNaughton's."

"How should I know?"

"But what do you think?"

"You said already you didn't *want* to go. You don't need me to help you make decisions like that."

"I know," said Frances, "but I'm feeling a bit guilty."

"There's no need," said Jack. "I mean, for all she knows you really do have an appointment in the city. It's quite reasonable. It's short notice, after all."

"I know," said Frances. "Yes, you're right. O.K., I won't go."

"Jack," Frances said uneasily as she spread the mayonnaise on their lunchtime sandwiches, "maybe I should."

"Should what?"

"Go to Ardelle McNaughton's party."

"Oh Jesus, Fran, what's the matter with you? Are you just getting the curse?"

"No."

"I mean, you're not usually like this. It's just a goddam Tupperware party. You don't want to go, so don't go. Do some work, for a change. Earn some money."

"But I feel really bad about it. I don't understand. I don't think I'll feel right until I tell her I'll go. I mean, it was really nice of her, wasn't it? She's trying to include me in things. Maybe she's giving it just for me."

"Oh God. Well, go then."

"Yes, I think I will. I'll call her right now." And Frances marched purposefully for the phone to call Ardelle McNaughton and accept.

The same group were there as had been at Gina Bombolinis, with a few additions ("Ask some other people," advised Mrs. Van Raalte. "For cover. You can always get rid of them."). There was a younger relation of Ardelle's, a stout matron whose young baby lay on a blanket on the floor at her feet. It engaged at intervals in massive, gurgling spit-ups which each time precipitated clucking of maternal dismay and noisily interruptive trips to the bathroom which threatened, thought Frances, to prolong the dismal ordeal almost indefinitely. (Why, why, *why* had she come? She had regretted her decision the minute she walked through the door.)

There were two harassed mothers, whose pre-school children fought with rising volume in the family room, and now and then erupted through the door with whining violence.

There was a heavyset older lady who was Somebody's mother. Her purple-tinted hair coordinated well with her purple crocheted sweater and purple capris, white ankle socks and lavender pumps. And there was the Tupperware Lady herself, whose stomachs protruded like shelving above and below the too-tight waistband of her black stretch pants, standing proudly in front of a table laden with brightly colored plastic objects and a few hygienic, indestructible children's toys. She clasped her hands across her pudgy middle, and exclaimed with a horrible enthusiasm: "I declare there's so much that's new that's exciting this month, I just don't know where to begin!" But having begun, she continued, with intermittent breaks while the evil-smelling baby was carried to the bathroom ("We don't want her to miss a thing, do we, girls?") for an hour and a half. Frances' jaw began to ache with the constant smiles and exclamations of insincere wonder as each object was picked up with reverence and its seemingly unlimited uses described at great length (the very same gadget, she discovered, could be used for cleaning around the inside rims of jelly jars, slicing orange peel, and made a pretty doily holder when upside down—"Incredible," cried Frances), and when someone pressed a glass into her hand she drained it and immediately accepted another, even though she never usually touched martinis. And, endlessly, the mobile arguments of the children in the family room:

"Mom, Arlene hit me in the stomach."

"Well, Leroy said I was a doo-doo."

"Leroy, you come right here to Mom."

"No."

"Leroy, come to me right now or you get a spank."

"She hit me *first.*"

"Arlene, that's not being Mommy's little lady."

And, demure in red and white frilly spotted dress and pink ribboned braids: "Leroy's a fucker," said Arlene.

Which Frances decided was the only bright moment of a dreadful morning.

There was a flurry of twittering activity over the departure of the Tupperware Lady and all her goodies. Arlene and Leroy were herded, whining, into almost identical station wagons. The baby, face shrouded in a clean diaper, was strapped into a foam car seat like a funnel, and Somebody's mother squeezed behind the wheel of her Lincoln Continental and Frances never knew whose mother she was.

"And now," Ardelle said happily, "let's us all have a little freshener upper."

"I'll buy that," said Gina. "Well, girls, wasn't that fun?"

And Rosemary Shapiro, having long ago left the group in spirit if not in body to return to her hazy never-never land, showed signs of returning animation. She rose to her feet in a series of jerks and, wordlessly, handed her empty glass to Ardelle.

"It was just great," said Frances. "Thanks for asking me. But I have to be running. . ."

"But Fran!" Ardelle's prominent blue eyes widened in dismay. "You *can't* go. I've made this special lunch."

Gina Bombolini wrapped a ponderous arm around Frances' shoulders. "Of course she can stay. Can't you, Fran?"

But Frances said firmly: "That's really nice of you, Ardelle, but I don't think so—Chetty comes home on the bus at 11:45. I'd better be getting on back *right now*."

It seemed there was no escape, however, for Gina said, in tones which brooked no interference at all: "That's fine. Connie stayed home today with a little bit of girl trouble. She can meet Chetty at the bus stop and walk her right on back to our house and give her a sandwich.

Don't worry about Chetty, Fran, she'll be O.K. I'll go and call Connie right away—she's sure to be fine again by now."

"Oh, well—" Frances said weakly (Chetty would be furious). Gina waddled resolutely for the telephone, and Frances sank back into her chair with, miraculously, a fresh drink in her hand.

Joanie Spritzer said: "Isn't that little Arlene a cute kid? I could just eat her up. Always dressed up so nice, and all."

And Ardelle said: "I guess now Sue's divorced she doesn't have too much else to do. Just buys new outfits for Arlene."

"Ah," sighed Joanie with envy, "divorce. Just think of it. The freedom. Sometimes I get real jealous of people like Sue. Especially when I think it all over; who I could have married, and all. I was pinned four times," Joanie told Frances, "and engaged twice. Three times, if you count Ben."

"I suppose you should," said Frances. "Count Ben. I mean, you married Ben."

And Joanie shrieked with shrill laughter. "Did you hear that girls? Honest, Fran, you just kill me! What a sense of humor!"

Frances looked puzzled (she'd said something *funny*?).

"Sometimes you wonder," continued Joanie, "looking back, if you'd do the same thing again. The others," she said nostalgically, "were nothing like Ben."

Barbara Woods asked very casually: "How about you, Fran? Is Jack your type? Physically, I mean?"

"Oh, tell, tell," cried Joanie gustily. " I love gossip."

Frances said crossly: "What kind of a question is that supposed to be?"

There was a small diversion while Rosemary Shapiro dropped her glass and searched for it under the chairs on hands and knees. Ardelle went to the kitchen to prepare a fresh pitcher of martinis.

Gina said: "She's only asking were all your men friends tall dark handsome Irishmen? She didn't mean anything personal."

Relax, Frances told herself, don't be so defensive. So she laughed and said: "I don't suppose he is my type, really. Both times I nearly got married before, they were blonde. Swedish-looking. Actually, one was German."

"No kidding," said Barbara. "In New York?"

"Well, no," said Frances. "One in New York, one here. In San Francisco. How do you know I'm from New York?"

"You said, didn't you?" Gina Bombolini asked of the room. "Didn't she say she was from New York, girls?"

"Yes, you did," said Barbara.

"Ah," said Frances muzzily, "Maybe I did. You're right—I remember."

And Joanie said: "You found a husband in San Francisco. That's amazing. Everyone unmarried over thirty in San Francisco is gay." And added darkly, "Or else has *problems*."

"Well," said Frances. "I just got in under the wire, then, didn't I? I caught Jack when he was twenty-nine. Before he turned gay."

Gina said: "Fran, I used to know a handsome, blonde German—a long, *long* time ago—it must have been ten years. What was his name, dear, anyhoo?"

63

Rosemary Shapiro abruptly abandoned her search. She cried: "No."

"Oh, Rosemary!" snapped Ardelle.

"For heaven's sake," said Barbara.

"It's not important," said Rosemary. "You don't have to tell them if you don't want to."

"But why shouldn't I?" asked Frances, looking bewildered. "I mean, what can it matter?"

"Everything," said Rosemary, and as the other five women in the room turned as one to stare at her, she bit her lip, flushed, made a small choking sound and left the room at a shambling run.

"Every time I see her," said Frances, "she's running out of rooms."

Eleanor said: "She's impossible. She gets worse all the time."

"Poor Rosemary," said Gina.

"Pathetic," said Joanie.

"What were you saying, Fran?" asked Barbara, "before Rosemary interrupted you?"

"Oh," said Frances. "Oh, yes. My friend—"

"His name, dear," said Gina. "I'm just dying to know if it could be the one I used to—"

"Dieter Sachs," said Frances. "He's a musician. Or he was a musician."

"No," said Gina. "Not the same. I never knew a Dieter."

"So, tell us," said Joanie. "Did you leave him for Jack?"

"Well, no I didn't," said Frances, half amused. "I left him just for himself. It got rough."

Joanie leaned forward, eyes bright with prurient expectation. "You mean—in bed?"

"Joanie," said Gina warningly, as Frances

flushed and looked annoyed, "that's none of your business."

"Fran, forgive me," said Joanie. "But you've had such an interesting life. I didn't mean to pry, though. I guess I got to running off at the mouth again, 'specially after a couple of drinks." She sighed. "But I wish Ben had a couple of bad habits. Ben's so bland."

"Not like Dieter," Frances said firmly. "Dieter was a lush. I guess he's still a lush. If he's still alive, that is."

SEPTEMBER 16

The tall man with the weak mouth and thinning yellow hair gratefully accepted the offer of another drink from the kindly, rotund little doctor seated on the bar stool beside him. "Thanks," said Dieter Sachs. "I could sure use it."

They had become acquainted over the first drink—it was actually only the doctor's first drink; Dieter had spent much of his day in Lenny's Hideaway on McAllister Street, and had long ago lost track of his own intake. Lenny's was a kindly place where fortune sometimes smiled. Dieter smiled now over the rim of his glass, vaguely in the direction of his new friend, wondering whether this promising new relationship would continue to bear fruit. It seemed it might; the small doctor was disconsolately preparing to drown some new sorrows, and so, quite possibly, some of Dieter's along with them.

"She up and walks out," he said bitterly. "I'd bought the goddam diamond and all. From Shreves. Cost a fucking fortune."

It never occurred to Dieter to wonder what a doctor who spent a fortune for a diamond from Shreve's was doing in a place like Lenny's. He sympathized in a maudlin drone: "That's too bad. But I guess that's women for you. Something comes along they think's better, they drop you flat."

Gordon Spriggs gazed mournfully at Dieter through his thick glasses.

"Flat," Dieter repeated.

"You sound like you've been along the same road, friend."

"Well—" Dieter thoughtfully swilled a long draught of bourbon around his back teeth, looking ready to confide. "Well, maybe. But it was a long time ago."

"And best forgotten," said Gordon Spriggs.

"Right," said Dieter. "Best forgotten. Forget the whole damn thing."

"Have another drink."

"Sure," said Dieter. " 'Nother drink. Know what? You're a real friend. Should be more people inna world like you."

"Bartender. Two more."

They drank.

"Know what?" said Gordon Spriggs. "I'll never forget. No, man, she just took off. Know what?" He leaned forward to murmur in Dieter's ear: "Said I drank too much."

"No kidding? That's just what Fr—Fran said. Eight—maybe ten years ago. Then I got married. And divorced. Can't remember what

66

my wife looked like—forgotten her goddam name. Forgot her goddam birthday," Dieter said proudly. "Gave me hell. Then kicked me out—Goddam bitch really ripped me off, too. I'm telling you, those laws are the shits . . . Jesus, was I ever screwed . . . Took every fucking thing . . . lucky to get out of it with my fucking *fiddle* . . . Goddam lawyers, they do O.K. *Screw* you, and do just fine . . ."

"That's real tough," Gordon said hurriedly, in an attempt to stem this dangerous new trickle of reminiscence which threatened to become a flood. "But you *remember* her."

"Yes," sighed Dieter, "I sure do. I'll never forget Fran. Shit, no. Never forget Fran."

"Me neither. Never forget that Mary."

Dieter raised his glass. "To Frances and Mary, wherever they are. Fuck 'em."

"Fuck 'em," said Gordon, then: "But you know, maybe I'm better off."

"Yeah?" asked Dieter politely, his eyes vague.

"Mary was cold. Beautiful, mind, but a cold woman. Didn't know how to please a man, if you follow."

"Sure," said Dieter. "Sure I follow. Not stupid." He began to giggle at his glass. "That's ir—irony, man." He shook his head. "Oh, Jesus, is that ironic? You know, that Fran?"

Gordon looked attentive.

"That Fran—just too much woman. Hard to handle." He lowered his voice. "Sometimes in the sack, just too much. And I'd have a drink or two, now and then, and I wouldn't be— wouldn't be able to—" Dieter looked about to cry.

"I know, man, I know." Gordon gestured to the bartender. "So she liked it, eh?"

Dieter took a long pull at his new drink. "Liked it? Jesus, man, she *loved* it. Had to have it. Every night . . . two, three times," said Dieter, his face puckering. "And I couldn't—"

"Wild, huh?"

"You said it, man. Wild woman. Kinky too."

"Is that so?"

"Yeah. Course, not now. Nothing kinky now. Ever'body does it," said Dieter in a fuzzy voice.

"Does what?"

"Ever'body."

"*What* do they do?" demanded Gordon, wanting to hit him.

But Dieter merely shook his head sadly while his voice trailed on into unhelpful, half-incomprehensible rambling. Dr. Spriggs thrust a dollar bill into his hand, saying: "Take this, friend. Buy yourself another." God*dam* the man. He rose. "Take care now," Gordon Spriggs told Dieter.

Dieter nodded. "Thanks, friend." His fingers splayed over the bill, but he never looked up.

"A tall blonde guy," Dr. Spriggs said into the telephone. "Seedy-looking. Real loser. On the booze hard. Knew our Frances ten years ago. Probably attractive enough then . . . it was kind of dark, though."

"Ah," said Mrs. Van Raalte.

"And Frances is reputedly a wild, kinky woman."

"Interesting," said Mrs. Van Raalte. "Do we know her—ah—particular bent?"

"He didn't say. He'd had just one too many. But bear in mind that to a drinking man, almost anything is kinky except a bottle. Should I try him one more time?"

"Better drop it," said Mrs. Van Raalte. "We have something to go on, now. That was quite well done, Gordon."

"But with another drink or two—that man wouldn't remember *anything*."

"We can't afford the risk," snapped Mrs. Van Raalte. "There must be no indication whatsoever that anybody was interested in Frances Driscoll."

"As you wish," said Gordon. "But could I ask what all this has to do with the child?"

There was silence at the other end of the line, and for one moment he thought she would hang up on him. But eventually she said: "To have access to the child, we need the mother. And knowing Frances' particular weakness, I shall provide her with a lover to indulge it. Since I shall be in direct control of this lover, I shall also be in direct control of Frances. You understand?"

"So far," said Gordon. "But she has a husband. What about the husband?"

"The least of our problems," said Mrs. Van Raalte. And he knew he would be told nothing more.

CHAPTER FIVE

September 16

"You can drop your donation through the slot, ma'am, and leave your envelope in the basket for Dr. Rossi," instructed Liam. "Hi, Mr. Dreyfus, how's it going?"

Mr. Dreyfus skipped nimbly by on his soft-soled, suede desert boots, an elfin, gray-bearded artist who lived with three teen-aged female ballet dancers on a houseboat down the dock. "One day soon," Florence said with a shake of her head, "that man is going to drop dead in his tracks. Just drop dead." Now, Mr. Dreyfus, much alive, smiled at Liam with a smile of gentle beauty and said: "Well, thanks, Liam. Going well." He wandered through the doorway into the comfortable room to perch expectantly in the front row on one of Florence's folding metal chairs.

The room was filling up, and at five minutes past two, Florence made her customary dramatic entrance, swooping through the expectant congregation like a vast green bat.

"Our Father, which art in Heaven,
Hallowed be thy name . . ."

Florence began with her customary prayer, necessary to cloak her activities with organized religion in order to satisfy the law.

Thy kingdom come . . ."

Liam edged onto the chair closest to the door, ready to slide unobtrusively out as soon as the prayer was over. He never tired of listening to Florence recite the Lord's Prayer.

"Thy will be done . . ."

Idly he wondered, as he always did, why this room—the comfortable room—should be so different from the rest of the houseboat. So bleak and so awful, thought Liam with distaste, eyeing the plastic flowers and the black-and-white cherubs, the tinted photograph of kittens in a basket and the gaudy imitation Indian rug. "It clears the air," Florence might have told him had he asked her. "I can pick up so much better because there's nothing of me around to distract me."

"On Earth as it is in Heaven.
Give us this day our daily bread,
And forgive us our trespasses . . ."

Trespasses. Liam thought of Jack, and he prayed, without much conviction: "Would You be able to help me love my brother?" and, guiltily: "Would You help me stop loving my brother's wife?" For over the past weeks his feeling for Frances had shifted once again, to something deep and troubling, and he found himself dreaming some very unsettling dreams

71

at night. "Forgive me my trespasses," whispered Liam. "Oh, please." He glanced around him for reassurance. The people were all very ordinary, and no one was looking at him. There were the usual half-dozen or so finely dressed middle-aged black women, some wearing spectacular hats. There were pale, frightened-looking girls and a scattering of suburban housewives. Then there were the regulars, including Mr. Dreyfus, come for advice in the handling of his one-man show in Los Angeles, and the paunchy dark-jowled man in the well-cut suit who Liam knew was a partner in a Montgomery Street stockbroking firm in San Francisco.

"As we forgive those who trespass
    against us.
And lead us not into temptation . . ."

Liam had always wondered why it should be necessary to ask *God* not to lead one into temptation. It seemed wrong. Once he had asked his brother, Pat, but Pat only said temptation was necessary as a discipline, in order to overcome one's baser urges. Liam had not understood. Pat was never any help; he always accused Liam of mockery, and refused to explain anything, ever since Liam, aged eight, had asked him what God had been doing before the Creation. Eventually, in despair at all the inconsistencies, Liam had thrown up his hands on his religion, for what terrors could the everlasting punishment for mortal sin ever hold for him when he already carried a living hell around in his head?

"But deliver us from evil . . ."

Liam decided, with defiance, that immediately after Florence's dramatic windup, he would go to San Rafael and see Frances. They could have a beer together on the patio, while Chetty played behind the fence in the new sandbox, unseen but cheerfully audible. Thinking of Frances in the sunlight, against the background of flowers, Liam's heart skidded to a momentary wrenching stop in his chest, and he clutched himself, smiling fiercely while listening to the violent pumping of the blood through his body, which amazingly had never missed a beat.

> "For thine is the Kingdom,
> The power and the Glory,
> For ever and ever . . . Amen."

Liam loved those lines. He would roll the words sonorously around his tongue: "The power and the glory, for ever and ever." What confidence, thought Liam. What fearless certainty. But today he barely listened, and before Florence unclasped her hands, opened her eyes and drew the first billet from the basket, he had slipped away soundlessly through the door.

Frances watched the arrival of the striped car from the living room window. She had been driven inside by the heat, and the living room was blissfully cool and restful, so that the Chrysler glared the more eye-achingly under the fierce early afternoon sun, its colors undimmed even beneath a thick layer of Waldo Point dust. She watched Liam climb from the front seat with very mixed emotions. Ever since Jack's outburst she had found everything in her life to be slightly shifted; her pivot point

73

was moved and her balance unsettled. And the innocence in her relationship with Liam was lost, as she had guessed it would be.

However, thought Frances reassuringly, at least he'll never know. There's no way he'll ever know; not unless Jack tells him himself what he said, and Jack would never dare.

Liam walked toward her across the graveled driveway, serene and unruffled in the heat, tidy as always, planting his feet lightly and deliberately, his body moving with grace and control. No longer a *kid* brother-in-law. Frances watched him with mingled anticipation and resentment, worrying about the self-control to be practiced and the careful deception, and the new relationship to be built from a quite new foundation so that Liam would never guess, for one moment, how her feelings had changed. Jack, Frances thought fiercely, if you'd kept your stupid insensitive mouth shut and left things alone, everything would be perfect like it was before. We were all so happy. And she wished suddenly that this was not the one day when Chetty had been invited out for the afternoon.

She said: "Hi, Liam. Come on in where it's cool. How are you?"

"Fine," said Liam. He settled his lean frame comfortably into the corner of the sofa among the cushions, accepting with pleasure the icy beer Frances offered him, "Jesus, Fran, I could drink a whole case." The car had been an oven, the steering wheel so hot he had scorched his hands, and now he held the frosted can gratefully against his burning face and looked at Frances. "So, what's new?" Outside, a sudden gust of hot wind whipped the oak leaves across the patio with a dry rustle.

"Nothing much," said Frances, "except, as Jack would say, the neighbors have been coming through."

"Again?"

"And again." And Frances briefly related the high points of the Tupperware party. "I thought I might write a few pieces on suburbia from the fresh viewpoint of one who's never been there—but I can't seem to settle into anything right now."

"Well," Liam said dubiously, "perhaps it's all a bit too peaceful for you." And remembering Frances' encapsulated summary the week before (". . . like a pink Goodyear blimp with a moustache . . . two forty-year-old Barbie dolls, sprayed and coordinated like crazy . . . an alligator in sensible shoes . . . Joanie something who dresses like a hooker . . . oh, and Rosemary Shapiro. She drinks . . ."), he added, "Those neighbors don't exactly sound the most stimulating group around."

"They're nice, though," said Frances dutifully, "and awfully kind."

"But you don't want to see too much of them," Liam said cautiously. "I mean, they seem like a real friendly group, but, oh *man* . . ."

"I know," said Frances. "Boring. But right now, I seem to have an infinite capacity for boredom."

"Been into the city this week?"

"No. Not once. I don't know why not. There's so much going on right now, but everything seems so easy here."

"And you haven't done any work."

Frances grimaced. "I guess I'd better get off my butt or I'll turn into a suburban zombie. I can see how it happens, now. It's like a creeping disease—there's just no incentive. You know, I find myself asking myself: Why make things complicated when they don't have to be. It scares me."

"It's unreal," Liam said.

Frances looked at him. "Yes," she said slowly. "Quite unreal. I was just going to say that," and something inside Frances squirmed as Liam's yellow eyes looked at her carefully. But he said nothing. He sat quietly and drank his beer, wondering why she was so edgy with him. For the first time in several weeks Chetty was not there, and although normally her presence was immaterial, today Liam knew Frances would have been more relaxed had Chetty been in the house. He tried to still his mind, to receive without searching, trying to find a reason. Frances did not want him to leave, he was sure, but neither was she completely glad he was there.

"How's Florence?" asked Frances.

She had never asked how Florence was. "Fine," said Liam. "Going on as usual."

"I can imagine what it must be like down at Waldo Point today; it must be absolutely wicked. It must be about one hundred degrees. One of those days when one shouldn't live on mud flats."

"Right," Liam said automatically, thinking: I could be a stranger. What is this?

And for the first time in her life Frances found herself needing to make conversation—with Liam, she thought in amazement. This would never have happened before; remembering with sadness how two weeks ago they would have talked and laughed together, quite unself-conscious, or if Liam had been uncommunicative, as he sometimes was, she would have gone about her own business, leaving him either to play with Chetty, or drink his beer alone.

That was why he came.

"Are you just here to visit, Liam," Frances asked inanely, "or is there something on your mind?"

"Should there be?" Liam asked. "I just felt like stopping by is all."

"Liam's mind?" Pat had once said with a degree of cruel satisfaction to old Mrs. Driscoll (as a Man of God, Pat never understood why people would confide, whenever possible, in Liam rather than in him. It wasn't right). "I'm afraid there's not very much on Liam's mind these days. You have to face up to it, Ma; perhaps Liam *had* potential, but he's wasting himself. To waste God-given talents is a wicked sin. I pray for him to change his way of life, and the company he keeps. I try, Ma. Only God knows I try."

Mrs. Driscoll had sighed, saying automatically: "You're such a comfort, Pat," thinking involuntarily of how much more of a comfort it would be to hear Liam's light step in the hallway instead of Pat's sanctimonious plod; to feel Liam's—Mrs. Driscoll was unable to phrase the word *compassion*, but she knew what she meant. Pat was well meaning, but occasionally she found herself wondering whether he did not suffer from the sin of pride; and even jealousy, thought Mrs. Driscoll

77

with unaccustomed insight. To her dismay, she found herself quite angry with Pat, and him a priest and far beyond her reach. But he was still her son, even though it was hard now to remember Pat as a baby. He seemed to have been born already adult and saintly, in his black shirt and white collar. Liam, now, had been a darling baby; so different from the others, but so warm and clinging. "You always loved Liam the most." Pat's pre-priest voice, the ringing resentment still clear after so many years. "You always loved him best."

Now, please God, let me not have upset Frances, thought Liam. I couldn't bear it. I must have *somebody*. He studied her carefully. She looked the same. Beautiful: thick black hair tied back in the heat with a green ribbon. A striped green-and-white sleeveless top worn over white shorts. Barefooted. Frances always looked good, her hair always shining, her body well cared for. She wore no makeup; her face was tanned and healthy, but when she smiled at him, there was a difference. It was a nervous smile, her eyes were not right, and when she spoke there was a forced note to her voice, although so slight he doubted anyone would notice but him. He knew Jack would never notice.

"Chetty will be back in about an hour," said Frances.

"Fine," Liam smiled. "Maybe I'll wait and see her," thinking: that must make it three times she's told me when Chetty's coming back. Why does she feel she has to tell me? Why can't she just relax, like always?

This isn't going well, thought Frances. I guess I'm a bad actress. If only she did not have to be alone with Liam. If only Chetty would come home early; and most of all, if only Liam was squat and ugly and fat, or had acne; was dirty, smelled bad, had dirt under his fingernails—something, anything, just so long as he was unattractive in some small way. Everything Jack had said was too much to the front of her mind, and this encounter with Liam too private. Also, somehow, he had picked up on her uneasiness right away.

"What's wrong, Fran?" Liam asked, giving her the chance to tell him if she wanted.

"Nothing. Everything's fine," said Frances.

"You're sure?"

"Sure I'm sure."

"You seem uptight today, that's all."

Frances laughed and fingered the ribbon at the back of her head. "It's only the heat. I didn't sleep well. It stays so hot at night."

"O.K.," said Liam. "If you say so. But— Fran, I feel I—I feel that there's something wrong with us. Something seems changed. I don't know—"

"Oh, Liam, you nut. You're crazy," laughed Frances. She jumped from her seat. "Have some more beer. What about a cookie? I made some yesterday. And Chetty will probably be back in a—"

Liam looked up at her sharply. "Sit down, Fran."

She sat down.

"Fran, look at me." He paused, then: "It's Jack," he said suddenly. "It's something Jack said, isn't it? What did he say, Fran?" He watched her eyes widen, and right away he knew what Jack had said.

"I don't—I don't know what you mean."

79

"I come over too much."

"Oh no!" cried Frances, flushing. "No. I *want* you go come. Chetty and I, we both—"

"He's right," Liam interrupted.

"My God," said Frances, "he told you! I could kill him. What a dumb, mean thing to do . . ."

Liam shook his head. "No. He didn't tell me anything. I haven't spoken to him in weeks."

"Liam, please don't stop coming or anything just because you feel that Jack—"

"But that's not all," Liam said.

"I'm sure," Frances said in a high-pitched voice, "that I don't know what you mean." She still stood, and now shifted her weight from one foot to the other, guiltily; found herself staring down at his hand and forearm as his fingers drummed lightly on the leather coffee table; really noticing for the first time the strong fingers, the copper hairs glinting healthily on bare, well-muscled arms; the light red-blonde stubble on his pointed chin—Liam had forgotten to shave—and fought an impulse to reach out her hand and touch his face, touch the thick mass of dark red hair which curled about his ears.

Liam raised his head with a jerk; his face was naked. "Fran, I *want* you to touch me."

"Oh Liam," said Frances, "please—please don't—"

Liam made a small sound of exasperation. It was suddenly too much, and the carefully built up restraints of years crumbled like the flaking dust of Waldo Point. It was the heat. The beer. The closeness of Frances. Her sudden new awareness of him. "Please don't what?" asked Liam. He rose from the sofa, his new beer untouched; he moved deliberately toward her as Frances backed against the marble mantel.

He rested a hand each side of her head, palms flat to the wall, leaning over her—he's taller than I expected, thought Frances. Then "Fran," Liam said, "take that thing off your hair."

Frances untied her ribbon with shaking moist hands, eyes still trapped by his. Her hair fell thick and soft around her shoulders; she could feel the heavy heat of it on her neck. Liam's face was pale, his nostrils pinched, but his eyes were hard and quite calm. For a few seconds he did nothing save twist one lock of her hair between forefinger and thumb, but that one small contact was enough for Frances to know the moment when his body tightened and tensed, deciding for him, and moved upon her, twisting his hands through the thickness of her hair at her neck, melting his every muscle, every tendon, and every bone into hers, and his eyes, inches from hers, shining gold, and inside her head, twisting . . . "Oh, Liam," said Frances, and her lips barely moved. His arm was tight around her in support; his face bent to hers. Liam kissed Frances in a way in which no inexperienced boy would kiss. "So he *has*, before," thought Frances giddily as her eyes closed, her body melted and her mouth opened under the strength of Liam's tongue. She groaned in her throat, compulsively dragging his hips against hers, forgetting Chetty, Jack, or that she and Liam could be plainly seen by any visitor passing by the window. Only Liam was real for her, reawakening wild, long-forgotten feelings which she had been so certain were tamed and buried under layers of habit, safety and control.

"I'd forgotten," cried Frances, "how wonderful—" and suddenly, shockingly, he was out of her arms. She half staggered, arms still outstretched, dropping them futilely at her sides. Liam stood back from her, mouth half open, clawing at his throat with one hand as though to unbutton his already open collar and give himself air, his body still powerfully aroused.

"Liam," Frances whispered, "Why? What is it?"

He stared at her. He had never seen her look like that. Her hair tangled and wild, her face soft and open, her body expectant. Liam dropped back into the sofa, every muscle aching. He dangled his hands loosely between outstretched knees, staring at his fingers, feeling ashamed, exposed and very vulnerable. Miserably, he cursed his brother for putting into words something which should never have been said. Just three stupid minutes, thought Liam, and he had spoiled everything.

"Oh Fran," said Liam, "I'm so sorry."

"Please, Liam, it doesn't matter."

"But it does." Then: "Oh my God; what am I going to do now?"

A few moments later, he left her.

"Oh no," Frances whispered, "Oh, no." She sank into the closest chair, knuckles pressed cruelly tight against the sides of her head, and gazed unseeing at her rounded brown knees. "Oh no; oh, please make that not have happened," for Jack had never aroused her as Liam had just done. And how had he known? So young; so inexperienced, surely. How had he known the precise way to approach her, to touch her, to hold her? As though they had been together countless times before. She closed her eyes and could still feel the hardness of his body against hers, the tight dense enfolding of his arms, the sharp edges of his teeth. Frances rubbed at her bruised mouth and moaned.

Liam pushed Florence's car back toward Sausalito at wicked speed. Fifty miles an hour he must be traveling, at close to a gallon of gas per mile. "Your power is entirely conscious and controllable," Florence had said, "right up in the front of your head." Or something like that. "I'd give anything," snarled Liam, "anything at all, anything in the whole *world* to lose this power. Do you hear me, God? Are you listening?" He swung too sharply around the off ramp past Marin City, rode the car up the shoulder, and was jarred and shaken as the huge body caromed off the edge of the curb and settled with an outraged thud back on the pavement.

The man driving the car behind him missed his left rear fender by inches. He rolled down his window to shout: "Get off the road, you fucking hippy."

Liam shook himself, and changed his plan. Now, he would take the car back to Waldo Point before he had an accident, and then hitch a ride into Sausalito, back to the No Name Bar, where he would get at least a little drunk, for he had five dollars.

CHAPTER SIX

September 21

The summer cooled to a late September of
misty mornings and early evening chills; a
slight but definite warning that fall was not
far off. Chetty played upstairs; Frances lay in
a garden seat on the patio, pretense at reading
abandoned, her face turned to the sun. Only
half awake, it took her several seconds to reg-
ister the significance of footsteps crunching in
the gravel driveway. She was expecting no
one; no one, that is, unless it was— Frances
sprang from her seat with a small chill of anticipation. She had neither seen nor heard anything from Liam since that day . . . only five
days ago, not yet a week, but it seemed forever. But it was not Liam. It was Rosemary
Shapiro. She stood back from the front door,
looking up at the house, her shadow long in
front of her.

Fighting the disappointment, hoping no
trace would show in her voice, Frances said:

"Come on in, Rosemary. It's nice to see you. I was going to make some coffee. Would you like some? Or a drink, maybe?"

"Vodka," said Rosemary, following her into the living room. "Straight."

"O.K.," Frances smiled. "I'll just go get some ice."

"Never mind about the ice."

"Just as you like," Frances said with slight impatience. "Are you walking?"

Rosemary said abruptly: "I wanted to see you. I didn't want to bring my car. People notice—"

Frances blinked. "You wanted to talk about something special?"

But Rosemary looked about her, at the pretty living room, the pictures, the shining floor, and the glowing rugs. "This is nice. You've made it look real nice."

"You've been here before? You knew the house when old Mrs.—uh—"

"Oh yes. When Mrs. Demetrios was here. I came sometimes." Rosemary watched anxiously as Frances took down glasses and the vodka bottle. "Why don't I do that? I know how I like it. I drink too much," she said suddenly. "I don't think I've been sober for years."

Frances asked: "Did you ever think of getting help?"

Rosemary looked at her. It was a curious look, Frances thought, almost of resigned scorn. "What's help?" She pointed to the half empty bottle and her almost drained glass. "That's help."

"But—*why?*" Frances asked weakly. "It won't do any good in the—"

Rosemary laughed. Her laugh was somehow

85

dreadful. "I started drinking after Don was killed."

"Yes, I heard that. But I didn't know he was killed, Rosemary. I thought he had a heart attack. When did it happen?"

"Four years ago," Rosemary said hoarsely. "Four years ago, about this time. October. Early October."

"Was it an automobile accident, then?"

"He had a stroke. That's what they said—a stroke."

"But I thought you said he was—"

"I mean, he died. What's the difference? He's dead, isn't he?"

And you're still grieving, after four years, thought Frances. I know it's sad, but it's morbid, after so long. You're killing yourself, Rosemary Shapiro. You're drinking yourself to death on *purpose*. She said: "Rosemary, I'm so sorry. I wish there was something I could say, but there never is anything, is there? Not that it'll help. One just has to go on living, doing the best one can, and—"

"I was away. In Los Angeles," said Rosemary, as though Frances had not spoken at all. "Don traveled, you know—he was on a trip, but he came on home while I was away. I don't know why. I found him when I got back. I don't know why he went home." Rosemary swallowed. "He'd been there a few days— three, they said—but nobody from the office had bothered to check. Just called, maybe, and when nobody answered . . . He made his own schedule when he was traveling. Furniture, you know. He was in furniture. Lovely line— just lovely furniture," Rosemary said vaguely. "He was looking at me as I went in, sitting in the armchair, with his face turned toward the door—it was hot, you know, like it's been—about ninety degrees. Indian summer."

Frances felt suddenly sick.

"They said it was a stroke. A clot in his brain. I don't know." Rosemary shivered. "It's cold in here, isn't it, Frances?"

"It is? It feels pretty warm to me." Frances checked the thermostat. "It says seventy-eight degrees. I hope you're not catching the flu."

Then: "He'd been there for days," Rosemary repeated. "And nobody looks that way unless—I mean, nobody's face, unless—"

"Unless what?"

"He was horribly afraid," said Rosemary in a whisper. And then, very fast, as though guessing her time was short: "Now you've got to listen to me, Frances. I like you. You're a nice person. You *must* . . ."

The front door bell shrilled through the empty house. Rosemary jumped in her seat; Frances flinched with shock, and the room grew suddenly darker.

The gigantic bulk of Gina Bombolini filled half the window. She stood outside in the front yard, smiling, waving to the women inside the living room.

"Don't tell her," said Rosemary urgently and soberly. "Don't tell *anybody*."

"But Rosemary," said Frances, bewildered, for everybody knew about the unfortunate Mr. Shapiro, "of course I won't, but why not? I don't understand."

"I've been baking," Gina said in the doorway, "and I brought up some cookies for Chetty. Hi, there, Rosemary, out walking? I

87

didn't see your car. That's nice. What *I* should be doing. Walking, walking, walking."

"I was leaving," said Rosemary, her voice shrill, making a strange empty gesture in the air as though pulling on an invisible coat. "Thanks for the drink. Good-bye, Gina."

They watched her walk fast and awkwardly down the driveway, her limbs queerly jerky as though attached to strings she remembered to manipulate only at the last moment.

"I guess she was telling you about Don," said Gina.

"Oh yes. Poor thing; I feel so sorry for her."

"She was never the same, after. Poor Rosemary," said Gina. "It hits some people that way."

SEPTEMBER 24

"So you're back," Florence said acidly. "Can you see if you can do anything with this kid?"

Liam stood in the door, pasty and hungover, looking down at the emaciated child Florence held in her arms. She was perhaps fourteen, barefooted, legs streaked with dirt and blood, face badly bruised and flea market dress ripped and stained. With a detached interest, he noticed a terrible boil on the side of the girl's neck under the unkempt, filthy hair. He noticed, too, her eyes, which bulged from her yellowish face in a torment of fear, her harsh shuddering gasps of breath, and her terrible smell.

"Christ," said Liam, "she's awful sick, Flo."

Florence passed her hand across the girl's hot forehead. "Goddam it, I *know* that."

"What's she on, Flo?"

Florence shrugged. "Everything. You name it, she's on it. Knocked up, too."

Liam squatted on the floor beside them, his head pulsing, his stomach nauseated, took the girl's thin, dirty-nailed hands in his own, and unwillingly looked up at her, trying to feel, trying to see. There were fleeting impressions of horror; he caught a glimpse of his own face through her eyes, twisted and wild with writhing lips like white worms. Then he said, "Easy, baby, easy. You're going to be O.K."

The girl began to scream, and Florence looked at him anxiously. "What is it, Liam? What's wrong?" Five dreadful minutes passed while the girl shrieked and tore at his eyes with her blackened claws, wrenching out of Liam's restraining grip with a fiendish strength almost impossible in one so debilitated. It was five awful minutes before she lay exhausted on the floor, the screams fading to muffled moans, "What's the matter," Florence asked. "Can't you do anything with her?"

"Not this time, I can't," said Liam, and angrily: "What did you expect? Why are you always leaning on me? I can't help her."

"Why not?"

"Fuck it, Flo, how do I know? It's not *there* any more. I can't see through into her, except for flashes. I can't reach out to her at all. And Flo," Liam said disgustedly, "you know something? I don't even want to. She makes me feel sick to my stomach."

There was a pause. They looked at one another across the body of the girl, who rolled her head from side to side and gobbled in her throat.

"Well," said Florence cautiously, "maybe if you wait a little it'll be O.K. You've been hitting the sauce too much; maybe tomorrow. . ."

But tomorrow was the same. He was sober and rested, and the images would not come.

Florence said: "I guess you've got what you always wanted."

And Liam thought with a chill that God must have listened at last.

SEPTEMBER 25

Frances sat shivering on a park bench, watching Chetty, the only child in the playground, as she rocked back and forth on a green and white painted plastic horse with handles jutting from the sides of its head. Chetty had already traveled every possible way down the slide and crawled up it backwards; ridden a plaster dinosaur, and built an unsatisfactory castle in the dry, crumbling sand. All that remained now, thought Frances thankfully, as the fog swirled around her, were the swings, and then they could leave.

Typical of coastal California, after weeks of blazing sunshine, the temperature had plummeted thirty degrees overnight, to coincide with the closing of the public schools for teachers' conferences. Not for the first time did Frances regret the absence of neighbors with small children with whom Chetty could have played, but at least the park was pretty and safe, even though cold as hell.

So now, said Frances to Frances, taking two sides, question and answer, as she was accustomed to do when faced with a problem, here is a time to review the current mess. A time for honesty. Something has happened; it must be faced and something done.

Question: Like what?

Answer: Nothing. Nothing can be done. My life has turned around, and the change will just have to be lived with and worked through. I'm not the same person I was two weeks ago, and now I'll have to readjust my relationships—with everybody, thought Frances with a chill.

Question: You can't lose total control one hot summer afternoon, and then expect everything to be the same, and to feel the same yourself, can you?

Answer: Oh, come on. Of course you can, decided Frances cynically, who had, over the past eight years been occasionally unfaithful to Jack without his knowledge, without being touched herself, and therefore with no harm done to anybody. But this time had been different—so different.

So what now?

What should she do?

How should she begin?

Jack unknowingly suffered for his outburst against Liam, for Frances now felt a new awkwardness in his company which was difficult to bridge with daily cheer. Presumably Liam suffered. Chetty certainly was miserable: "Mom, we haven't seen Uncle Liam in *too long*." Everybody suffered. "Dumb, oh, dumb," moaned Frances, torn by the need for action and the sure knowledge that there was absolutely nothing to be done.

Time would take care of everything, to a certain predictable extent, as it always did. At least, she hoped so. But it was cold comfort and no help for *now*. Given enough time she knew her own feelings would lose much of their sharpness. She might even grow to look upon this situation with the wry humor it surely deserved. Liam would undoubtedly find another woman and forget her—if he hasn't done so already, thought Frances with a stab of jealousy. Impatiently, she shook herself. She must get going again; she *must*. That was the first thing to do. Stop brooding, and pick up the telephone. Call some of her friends and make plans. See other people—"I've seen nobody for weeks," Frances realized with surprise.

She hugged her arms around her body, rocking back and forth in the cold. She had to get back to work. Start to think about other, more important things. She had still not begun to write again. "You'll finish the novel by Christmas," Jack had said. "You'll have all the time in the world." But, thought Frances, maybe I don't function at all except under pressure. Maybe I needed all that hassle. Perhaps I'm the type who goes to pieces when things get too quiet and easy; for she remembered that despite the constant other demands on her time she had always managed to write too. There had always, somehow, been time for everything, then.

Absently she watched an elderly hunch-shouldered man in a raincoat, also looking cold and thoughtful, hands thrust deep into his pockets, slowly making his way toward the playground through the rhododendron bushes. Chetty rocked back and forth on the plastic horse with a rhythmic squeal of unoiled bearings.

So get a grip on yourself, Frances told herself sternly. One change of lifestyle and you fall apart. A few weeks of country living, and you've turned into a neurotic, lazy klutz who messes up everybody's lives out of boredom. Get off your butt; think of all the good things you have now. A lovely house. A safe neighborhood for Chetty. A good school. Give it all a chance, at least. Work something out with Liam. It can be done. And for God's sake get back to work.

Frances shivered. Footsteps crunched down the gravel path as the man in the raincoat approached. The protesting squeak of Chetty's horse slowed, and finally stopped, as the man also halted on the path beside the playground, waiting in the fog—for his dog, thought Frances. Poor thing, having to exercise a dog in this weather. At least I don't have that—it's one less thing to have to worry about, and please God don't make Jack feel he has to get one now that we live out here. All I need is a puppy—although to be honest, it would be fun for Chetty and what else am I doing nowadays anyway? Sitting in the fog freezing to death watching her ride that goddam horse—thank God she's stopped for a minute, that noise was driving me nuts.

Chetty called out conversationally: "Mommy, I can see his wienie."

"His—" Frances blinked. For the last five seconds she had been gazing with unseeing concentration at an erect penis. The man stood not ten feet from her, his head thrown back, his raincoat opened to disclose the sagging brown pants, the gaping fly, and a long, skinny organ, curving upwards from its nest of grayish-brown hairs (Frances was close enough to count them, had she so wanted), brownish purple in color, red veined, with pale brown spongy tip. "Disgusting," said Frances.

Chetty looked with interest, saying pleasantly, "I've seen my dad's, too."

With face of stone, Frances said: "Chetty, come here right *now*. We're leaving."

The man stood and grinned at her.

"Go away," Frances said, "or I'll call the police."

"But Mom," Chetty protested, "I haven't been on the swing yet."

"Forget the swing. Just do as I say. We're going home right now. D'you hear me? Right now."

Frances began to shake. With a trembling hand she picked up her purse which lay beside her on the bench, and Chetty's coat. She tried to remember all she had heard about flashers. She must not react. Or speak to him. Try not to look disgusted, or frightened. She must walk slowly—slowly—"*Will* you come on, Chetty—" for the exit, where thankfully a car was stopping, to disgorge several small boys with a basketball. She must speak to their mother—to warn—but already the car was pulling out. "Hey," Frances called to the children, "hey, boys," but they had run far from her down the soggy grass, calling to one another, passing the

94

ball. "Oh, hell," Frances said. The man had gone anyway, vanished in a swirl of fog-colored raincoat, away up toward the tennis courts.

So safe in the suburbs, thought Frances. Yeah. Thinking: how ridiculous to be afraid of a flasher. What we'd have called a pervert. How we would have laughed if it had happened in the city. Curiously, she felt tears pricking behind her lids. She wanted to collapse onto her car seat and cry and howl, for his timing had been dreadful, but that would never do— keep one's composure before the kids. Chetty trailed behind her, resentment wearing a small plaid overcoat, grumbling about the swing.

"Never mind," said Frances. "Maybe next time. When that man isn't here." And rashly: "Maybe you can go with Uncle Liam."

SEPTEMBER 27

Of course Jack heard about it, for Chetty told him nonchalantly over Sunday breakfast. She had started to laugh, and choked in her orange juice, and Frances patted her between the shoulder blades.

"What's so funny?" Jack asked.

"Just thinking about that man."

"Man? What man?"

Frances said: "Chetty, what do you want to do today? Shall I see if somebody can come over and—"

"What man?" asked Jack.

When Chetty told him, he was very shocked, as Frances had known he would be. Something must be done, Jack said.

SEPTEMBER 28

On Monday evening, Jack was late home. The weather was fine again, and Chetty played outside after supper, riding her tricycle in the driveway. Frances cleared up the kitchen and began to make herself a drink.

When Jack's car eventually drove up, he did not get out at once. He responded to Chetty's overwhelming welcome, and Frances could see through the kitchen window that he showed her something inside the car. Their heads were bent close together, the back of Chetty's neck rigid with excitement.

."Mom? Oh, Mommy!" Chetty flew toward the house, crying: "Mom! Mom! Guess *what*? Mom, Daddy's brought me a puppy!"

"Oh, no." Frances almost stamped her foot. But she said: "That's lovely, darling. But please don't let it in the house."

Chetty said casually: "It's already in." Frances entered the living room in time to see the puppy squat on the best Bokhara rug and urinate. She was furious. "Oh, Jack, why? You *know* I didn't want a—"

"I thought we should have one," Jack said very seriously. "For protection. For you and Chetty."

"Hah!" Frances said skeptically. *"That's* protection?"

"It'll be very big when it's grown up, honey."

"It will? Oh, my God. What is it?"

"It's a Labrador," said Jack, "mostly."

Chetty decided at once to call the puppy Grover. Grover was male. His fur was a very pale cream. ("I thought Labradors were black," Frances said. "That's not even *mostly* a Labrador.") His stomach was soft, naked and pink and after a meal swelled like a balloon. He had a small tail, "like a rat," Chetty said, which in time would grow to be full and feathered. He had a fine head, silky ears and was altogether appealing, but Frances was unmoved. Before she had finished scrubbing the rug, Grover had made a small puddle on the hardwood floor. "Oh, *hell*," said Frances.

Chetty made a bed for him in an old grocery box. She lined it with comfortable rags, and placed it in the corner of the kitchen with a pile of newspapers in front of it which Grover never used. Neither did he sleep in his bed. For most of his first few nights at Woodburn Lane he howled and scratched at the kitchen door until either Jack or Frances came downstairs. He defecated everywhere but on his paper. And as she had known all along must happen, the ultimate care of Grover fell more and more to Frances.

"Oh, Mommy," breathed Chetty, "I think Grover really loves you."

And Frances frowned horribly at Grover who smiled brightly up at her, his little ratty tail wagging, one of Frances' shoes, $49.95 at

97

Saks Fifth Avenue, half gnawed between his front paws.

SEPTEMBER 30

In atonement, Jack set up Frances' typewriter for her, made her some bookshelves, and brought her a fresh ream of paper from the office. And with a feeling of resolution and virtue, determined to begin her novel at last (nothing should stop her, not even the dog) she marched into the living room to turn off the telephone. It rang in her hand.

"Coffee, Barbara? This morning? Well, I was actually going to—in half an hour?" Incredibly, she heard herself say: "Sure, that would be fine. I'd love to."

After all, what else did she have to do that was more important?

"Ben never wants to go out," complained Joanie Spritzer. "Just wants to watch T.V. Every night."

"Too bad," said Gina Bombolini. "And it's football season, too."

"I don't mind watching football," said Joanie. "I like big, husky men."

"Anyone would look big and husky; the padding, you know," Frances said vaguely. "Even Ben would look big and husky."

Joanie said: "Jack has a terrific build. He looks like he must have played football. You tell him from me he's real cute."

"O.K.," said Frances. "I'll do that."

"You and I, Fran, we must like the same kind of men."

Gina looked at Joanie sharply.

Frances said: "You think so?"

"Sure we do. We go for the big guys—"

"I suppose, but being quite tall myself—" Did this group *ever* discuss anything but men? thought Frances, strangling a yawn.

"Ben's always been real defensive," Joanie went on. "He's had this complex just about since he was born. About being skinny, you know. But at least he's tall."

"And so nice," Frances said politely.

"Oh sure," Joanie said casually. "No one could say Ben wasn't a real nice guy. Just not very lively, if you know what I mean. Wants to eat dinner and slump in the evenings. Though there're some good movies this fall. Last night we watched Robert Redford in—"

"Now, *he's* not tall," said Gina.

"I know," said Joanie, "but who *cares!* Great coffee cake, Barbara."

"Oh," Barbara said modestly, "I don't know. I guess it's O.K."

Frances' yawn escaped. She said quickly: "It's terrific. But I'll have to watch out. Don't let me have one more piece."

Gina said, the sugary crumbs plainly visible on her hairy upper lip, "Don't tell me that a toothpick like you is worrying about her figure."

"I suppose one must draw the line somewhere," said Frances.

"You have a long way to go," Gina said balefully, who today looked even fatter than usual, a billowing whale in pink polyester. "Eat and enjoy."

Barbara said: "Don't bully Frances, Gina."

And Ardelle said smoothly, returning the topic into its original channel: "Joanie, how would you describe your ideal man?"

Joanie settled at once into what Frances realized must be a well-worn groove. "A body like Victor Mature—"

Barbara said: "Too much of the beefcake."

And Gina said thoughtfully: "Oh, I don't know."

Which triggered a chorus of middle-aged housewifely voices. Only Eleanor Spriggs looked bored; bored but tolerant, thought Frances, who try as she might could not imagine Eleanor with a man at all. What must her husband be like?

"Blonde hair, blue eyes and a firm, determined chin," said Ardelle.

"Blonde with brown eyes," said Joanie. "I don't care about the chin."

"Blonde hair's nice," Frances said dutifully. "I like blonde men. With maybe green or hazel eyes."

"Interesting," Barbara murmured. "Unusual."

"And how about redheads?" said Joanie. "You know what they say about redheads?"

"No," said Gina. "What do they say about redheads, dear?"

Frances felt a telltale hot flush rising up her neck and seeping across her face from both ears. She looked quickly about the room, but nobody had noticed. However, she herself noticed something strange, and it took her several moments to realize what it was. Something was missing. Rosemary Shapiro. Rosemary Shapiro was missing.

". . . and a good tan," said Gina.

"Oh yes," Frances said eagerly, "a good tan."

"And what sort of nose?" asked Barbara. "Big nose? Thin nose? Hawk nose?"

"Not too big," said Frances (determined not to discuss redheaded men). "Well formed, quite thin. Maybe slightly hawkish on the bridge."

"Oh, sexy," gurgled Joanie. "And he must have a wide mouth with a sardonic smile."

Eleanor Spriggs spoke for the first time. "Joanie, you're reading too many trashy novels."

"No," said Joanie. "Just too much trashy T.V. And fabulous teeth." It needed more than a snide remark from a neighbor to stop her now.

"Of course," Frances agreed. "Fabulous teeth."

And Joanie said: "Fran, why ever did you marry Jack? Not that he doesn't have great teeth—"

Frances asked, her heart pounding, "Why do you say that? What do you mean?"

"Only that you've described your perfect man, and he's blonde and green-eyed, with a tan and a—"

"Well-formed thin hawk nose," Barbara added.

"Good grief," Frances protested, "are you ladies taking notes?"

There was a tiny, uncomfortable pause, and Joanie said quickly: "I mean, Jack's dark and blue-eyed, with that kind of skin that doesn't tan—"

"You're right," Frances said with a light laugh that hurt. "He's not my type at all, is he?"

CHAPTER SEVEN

October 5

"Student housing in Saudi Arabia? Jack, that's terrific! Saudi *Arabia?* How wonderful," Frances said very sincerely, realizing that soon there would be a period in her life without Jack—maybe for weeks, she thought hopefully, during which she would work everything out, solve every problem, shake herself from her disoriented lethargy and greet Jack on his return as the old, fun-loving Frances. He would write off her current mood as relocation blues, and never need to know there had been any other reason. "Jack, I'm so glad. It's really exciting."

"But I'll have to leave *soon*, Fran. Next week."

Wonderful.

"They didn't give you much warning, did they?" she said. "How come it's such short notice?"

"Well—it's a very strange thing, Fran. Epstein and Associates already had the contract, but the final papers hadn't been signed yet. And then, right at the last moment, they chose our proposal instead. There'll be a godawful mess about it. Nobody understands what happened, but obviously Epstein's greased the wrong palm, or made somebody mad somewhere; these Arabs are miserable to deal with. So it's ours—a sixty million contract. Imagine!"

"Sixty million," Frances said admiringly. "That's terrific."

"Student housing outside Jedda," said Jack. "Fran, you must come with me."

"Go with you? Jack, you're crazy. How would I do that?"

"Couldn't we swing it, Fran? I'll have to be away at least a month. I don't want to be away from you all that long."

"We couldn't possibly afford it. No way."

"I know we can't afford it, but shit, you only live once. And all of my expenses are paid, and the hotel—Fran, think about it."

"No, Jack. And what would I *do?* I'd be in the way ..."

"There'll be a pool in the hotel. There'll be shopping—"

"Oh, sure. And what about Chetty?"

"She could stay with somebody. Anybody would take Chetty. The Bombolinis would probably be glad to, then she wouldn't have to miss any school."

"But she *hates* the Bombolinis." Then Frances played her ace. "What about Grover?"

"Oh, fuck Grover. He can go into a kennel. Think about it, Fran? Please?"

"No, Jack. It's just too much of a hassle. And my passport's expired."

Jack looked at her, bewildered. "You don't *want* to go, do you? I mean, Chetty and Grover and your passport, those aren't reasons not to go. Those are excuses. I don't understand, Fran. A month ago—"

"I'd rather stay here and relax. Go to bed early; catch up with some reading. That kind of thing."

"Go to bed early? Why, are you sick?"

Frances smiled wryly. "You should be pleased. Maybe I'm settling down."

"Why should I be pleased? You've suddenly changed so much I just can't handle it. I married *you*, Fran. I want you the way you were." And he added resentfully: "And it's so quiet around here."

"But that's what you said you always wanted."

"I know; so I was wrong, right?" He had never thought he would actually miss Frances' friends. "You're a people catcher, Fran," he had shouted in despair so often in the past, "and the odder the better." (And the phonier, he had also groaned in darker moments.) But all these people, even the faggy designer, the pornographic movie director, and the peripatetic yachtsman who occasionally arrived at the door en route to Tahiti, Galapagos or Sydney, Australia, carrying a sack of fetid laundry, were far to be preferred over the inhabitants of Woodburn Hills. The neighbors had fallen disappointingly short of his expectations, but appeared amazingly to be taking over as Frances' sole companions.

And Frances seemed so placid. She never argued with him anymore, and she seldom went out except to the grocery store and to perform other small errands from which she came right back. He asked suddenly: "Fran, when did you last go to see—uh—Florence and Liam?"

"I don't know," she answered. "Not for weeks. I don't remember."

"Weeks." Frances used to take Chetty to Waldo Point at least once a week. And neither was Liam coming to the house. Jack knew he should be glad for this, but he was not. It was disturbing.

"—Something seems wrong to me. I mean, he's always here when I'm at work—he never waits to see me—it's like he's avoiding me. Liam's always been—I guess you'd just say 'different.' I wouldn't want to think that he was making any trouble . . ."

Jealous, Jack thought frankly. I was only jealous. Surely I never really believed that my own *brother* would . . .

Perhaps there lay the basis of all his problems—jealousy of Frances. Of charismatic Frances, the center of the group, whose appearance would revitalize the most boring party. Wherever Frances went, she brought fun and excitement, so of course Liam preferred her company rather than his. Thinking honestly, for a change—in fact with brutal objectivity—Jack wondered to what extent the move to San Rafael had been motivated by his own jealousy, intended to knock Frances out of her brilliant orbit? He felt shaken and guilty, certain that he had contributed his own share to this new, passive Frances.

He said: "Fran, what do you do with yourself all day?"

"I don't know," she shrugged. "I had coffee with Barbara Woods a few days ago—"

"Big deal."

"And I suppose I should probably give a lunch to repay all that hospitality."

"Whose hospitality? We haven't been anywhere—"

"The neighbors."

"Do you see anyone except the neighbors?"

"Jack, of course. What do you think I'm doing? Vegetating completely?"

Yes, thought Jack. And he complained: "We haven't even gone out at night except to something or other next door." And in the years gone by, Jack had grumbled so often: "Must we go out so much? Can't we stay home more?" Now he stayed home at night more often than not, and yes, he was bored.

"But we have," said Frances. "Of course we have."

"Only to a movie. And once to a restaurant for dinner. We haven't seen any of our other friends for nearly a month."

Haven't we? thought Frances, puzzled. I really meant to do something—surely we must have—but the days were slipping by; sometimes it would be time for Chetty to return at noon, and she would find herself still lying on her bed—and in my bathrobe, she thought guiltily, not even dressed—her only achievement the early feeding of Grover. What *had* she been doing? Where did the mornings go? She had still not written a word of her novel, and when the telephone rang it was sometimes too much trouble to answer it, and so it rang less and less.

She felt very tired. "Please, Jack, could we talk about it later?"

OCTOBER 8

Gina Bombolini said: "Wouldn't that be the answer? Let her go with him to Saudi Arabia? It would make everything so much simpler if Connie and I had the child."

Mrs. Van Raalte stared at her coldly. "Are you *mad?* The disappearance of the child must be attributed to her mother's negligence, not to yours."

"Oh," said Gina stupidly. "You're right. Of course."

"Naturally," said Mrs. Van Raalte. "And speaking of Connie, we shall be needing her. Very soon. It's time she joined us; she's a competent girl."

"Joined us? But how? We don't need her."

Mrs. Van Raalte smiled. Gina shivered, and wondered, not for the first time, how old she was. "Oh, yes we shall," said Mrs. Van Raalte, still smiling. *"Very* soon."

OCTOBER 13

The flurry of Jack's departure passed over Frances almost unnoticed. There were the dramatics invariably associated with his journeyings. Jack hated to fly; nerving himself up to strap himself inside what he considered nothing better than a multi-million-dollar metal coffin involved several sleepless nights, tranquilizers, belts of vodka, and major panics over temporarily mislaid wallet, passport, money, and air tickets. He insisted on reaching the airport at least two hours before flight time: "You never *know*, Fran. Anything could go wrong." And Frances amiably packed for him, and forgot nothing.

All the way to the airport he agitated loudly about hijackings, bombs, and the chances of botulism from the pre-packaged food. Frances handed him over to an associate from Koenig, Thomas and Driscoll, who marched him briskly off to the bar, after only the briefest farewell, and it was with a feeling of deep relief that she took the silent Chetty by the hand and returned to the parking lot. She swung onto Highway 280 for San Francisco, headed for Route 101 North, the Golden Gate Bridge and Marin County, with an imperative longing to be home on Woodburn Lane. For Chetty, who wept quietly beside her, she felt only impatience.

OCTOBER 14

"Hey, Fran. How'ya doing?"
  "Fine, thanks. Who—who's this?"

"Now, Fran! Honesta God! It's Marge, honey."

"Oh, Marge. Well, hi."

"Lissen, Jack said to give you a call and say hello. Said you'd not been feelin' too great, or somethin'. Why don'tcha come on over Friday night for supper with Mom and Dad?"

"Well—Marge, that's really nice of you. I'd just love it, but Friday night there's some kind of meeting at Chetty's school," Frances lied. "I missed the last one, and I really have to go to this one. Why don't I call you next week? Maybe we can get together later on. It'd be great seeing you and Kevin—"

"O.K.," said Marge equably. "Fine with me. Just so's we know you're all right."

"I'm fine," said Frances. "Honest. I must have had some kind of bug, but I'm all over it now. Tell Mom and Dad not to worry, and I'll bring Chetty over in a week or so. Listen, thanks for calling. I'll get back to you later. And say 'hi' to the kids for me."

OCTOBER 15

And so came the day Rosemary Shapiro died. Frances lay on the huge bed, staring out across the tops of the oak trees to the changing patterns of cloud reflections moving quickly over the water of the San Francisco Bay, remembering the first of July, and how she had been then. Thinking about how she was now, and wondering why but not really caring.

She listened to the telephone ring twenty, twenty-one, twenty-two times. "Give up," she said aloud, "whoever you are, because I'm not going to answer." But whoever was calling seemed to *know* she was there and at the thirtieth ring, Frances picked up the receiver.

"Frances, can we meet? I have to talk to you."

"Sure, Rosemary. When's a good time? Today's got kind of involved, but perhaps tomorrow—"

"Today, Frances. *Now.* Right now."

"I can't now, Rosemary. Chetty will be home pretty much any minute, and I have to make lunch, and—maybe this afternoon? Connie Bombolini's taking her to the park—"

"I'll come over to you. Now."

"But, Rosemary—"

Rosemary hung up with a click, and left vibrating silence. "Oh no," said Frances, angry at the intrusion. She would have to get up and get dressed now, although possibly Rosemary would be too far gone into her morning to notice she was still wearing a bathrobe. Frances sighed. Within five minutes she would hear the growl of Rosemary's poorly driven Karmann Ghia, the squeal of brakes, the splatter of flying gravel. And of all people today, she did not want to see Rosemary Shapiro.

"She was drunk of course," said Gina.

"I don't know," said Frances thoughtfully. "Not as drunk as usual. I mean, she was making sense; for Rosemary, that is." She began to shake. "Oh, God, I must have been the last person to ever talk to her. She was coming over to see me."

111

"What about?" Gina asked. "Did she say?"

Frances shook her head. "I don't know. It can't have been important, though. I didn't know her well. What could have been so important?"

"Now then, honey, you're not to worry yourself," Gina said comfortably. "Poor Rosemary was just drunk."

"But she didn't really sound—"

"Honey, alcoholics only sound sober when they're really plastered. Now just don't worry yourself. It had to happen sooner or later. It could have been worse, you know. This way, it was fast, and she didn't take anybody with her, either. Why, I'll bet she never even knew a thing about it."

"Terrible," said Joanie, "but Gina's right. We might have expected something like this to happen."

"Poor Rosemary," said Eleanor Spriggs. "Gordy and I warned her, but she wouldn't listen."

"She should have had counseling," said Ardelle.

"I said she should go to Alcoholics Anonymous," Barbara said piously. "They do a wonderful job."

"Self-destructive," Gina agreed, nodding wisely, "or she'd have done something long before this."

"Ever since her husband died," said Joanie. "Poor Rosemary."

"—never the same."

"—never seemed quite right."

"And we warned her," said Eleanor. "She never listened."

And Frances said, shivering: "If only I'd

gone to see her, like she wanted . . ." and began to cry.

OCTOBER 16

Florence said: "Someone was killed."

Liam said sullenly: "So?"

"A woman on Woodburn Hills Road," said Florence. "That's where—"

"Let me see." Liam took the afternoon *Independent Journal* from Florence, scanning the short brutal paragraph.

WIDOW DIES IN AUTO WRECK
Rosemary Shapiro, 45, was killed instantly this afternoon when her Karmann Ghia sports car was struck by a . . .

"It's a neighbor," Liam said. *"Was* a neighbor. Fran knew her." He looked away from the newsprint, suddenly dizzy, the words swimming sickeningly on the page.

Florence asked sharply: "Was she a close friend? Maybe you should go up there—it says here about the school bus, and the kids seeing it and all. It was noontime—that must have been Chetty's bus. You should go—"

"No," said Liam. "I'm not going up there. You don't understand—" He looked up at Florence with defiance, his face pale and greasy with sweat. He said: "Anyway, I'm not feeling good. I'm feeling sick to my stomach."

Florence said shortly: "You better take some Pepto-Bismol. You been hitting it too hard."

"Yeah," Liam said absently. "I know. And there's this headache coming, too." He still gazed down at the newspaper. "Funny," he said, rubbing at his eyes.

"What's funny?"

Liam looked up. "I don't know, Flo. I really feel weird. I'm going to go lie down."

"You do that," said Florence.

CHAPTER EIGHT

October 17

Mrs. Van Raalte sat at her desk in the living room. It was 2:00 A.M. The air was dense and very still, and below in the valley the freeway thundered and the monoxide-laden air vibrated, as produce trucks and an endless steel river of automobiles rumbled into the Bay Area from the northern valleys, the roar of their engines and the belch of their exhausts the heartbeat and breath of California.

The old lady sighed and blinked. Sometimes, like tonight, she remembered how old she was, when her eyelids smarted and leaked at the corners, her body ached and her skin felt rough and overly sensitive. Ready for the wrecker's yard, she thought grimly, unless something was done to halt the indignities and cruelties of time.

In front of her on her desk lay a heavy book, its pages sharply illumined by an angled lamp which also shone on Mrs. Van Raalte's old hands, which appeared to have been severed at the wrists for her forearms were in deep shadow. She sighed again, with something approaching satisfaction, for very soon she hoped to be reaping the fruits of years of labor. No effort would be spared now in the attack on Frances Driscoll, for traditional methods might not be enough. No, now that the family was disintegrating, the husband gone, the mother and daughter increasingly at odds with one another, so she heard, there remained two further moves, one originating with her, and which she considered nothing less than the stroke of a genius; the second, and more prosaic, with Gordon Spriggs. When everything had fallen into place, success was more or less totally certain, and Mrs. Van Raalte licked her lips.

Her part now was to find the right kind of face . . . and then assume battle stations, prepare herself for suspended days and nights of outpouring energy, the exhaustion—but for what a reward.

The book she studied was the Los Angeles Actors' Casting Directory, for it was better, Mrs. Van Raalte knew from experience, not to leave everything to the imagination, and she needed a particular face.

Her long pointed fingernail, with its plum-colored polish, tapped thoughtfully at the chin of the relatively unknown Bill Koeller. He appeared to be in his middle thirties; he probably was, as his age was not listed. He looked right. He had a good face, with clean-cut northern European bones. His hair was thick, straight, and probably naturally blonde. He appeared to have a good tan. His eyes were hazel. His nose was straight and thin, his mouth wide, firm, and humorous. A sensitive mouth, but strong. A good chin. Bill Koeller stood over six feet barefoot. Oh yes, thought Mrs. Van Raalte, he'll do, all right. Experimentally, she reached out toward him with her powerfully trained mind to test his susceptibility, for the essence of Bill Koeller had to arrive when called. And she gave him a new name, for he must have a name when presented to Frances. An untraceable name.

With a lugubrious twist of her mouth, she decided to call him Warren Pitt.

In Southern California, in the studio apartment in Los Angeles just off Wilshire Boulevard which was more expensive than he could rightly afford, Bill Koeller twisted and turned in hateful nightmare. He tried with desperation to scream, but knew he made no sound as he felt his head and shoulders forced downwards into suffocating darkness, and his knees double up to his chest. And he plunged, tumbling uncontrollably over and over, to reach at last a grinding metallic universe where he rushed forward, faster and faster, while twin glaring lights, one after the other, the eyes of a million monsters, swooped upon him and behind him at lunatic speed and a hot, poisonous wind, laden with stinging particles, beat brutally into his face to flatten his cheeks and wring streaming tears from his bulging, blinded eyes. And he continued to scream, knowing well that his screams were stifled in his throat or torn away uselessly from his lips into the hot, polluted wind . . .

Suddenly he was back in his own room. But

no longer inside himself. He was looking down upon his own body, and the feeling of panic was of different substance but equally unbearable. There he was. There *it* was. Apparently serenely asleep on the studio couch. Arms outstretched. Head turned to the left. Legs straight. The contours of the naked body plain under the single sheet. And then Bill was awake, shaking in terror, and the traffic of Wilshire Boulevard again pounded through the night only yards away through the wall of his building. Somewhere a siren screamed, human beings laughed and shouted as they left the discotheque across the street, and somewhere in the building came the reassuring sound of a flushed toilet. Bill Koeller sat up, watched his hands as they trembled, carefully lit a cigarette from the pack beside his bed on the bookcase which doubled as a night table, and smoked very methodically, drawing the smoke deep into his lungs, exhaling in gasps. "Jesus," he said aloud, "oh, Jesus."

He was afraid to lie down again and try to sleep, disgusted with himself for his fear. "A dream," he said, "just a dream." A nightmare. Nothing—but he was terrified that once again a corner would lift again, plunging him into that world of fear and chaos. But he had to be fresh for the morning's audition for the cigarette commercial. It was as good as his; he would be perfect. Morrie had told him so. And God only knew, he needed the money. Bill Koeller used the bathroom, took a sleeping pill, drank some water and returned to bed, reassuring himself that it was only a dream which couldn't hurt him. And until morning his sleep was undisturbed.

"Harper Investigations, good morning."

"Mr. Harper, please."

"May I tell him who's calling?"

"You may not."

"Just one moment, please."

Pause.

"Harper here."

"I have something for you, Harper."

Pause.

"It's been a long time."

"I know."

"I thought you'd—"

"Forgotten you? I wouldn't do that, Harper."

"No. No, I guess not. What do you want?"

"There's an actor. Bill Koeller. K-O-E-L-L-E-R."

"Never heard of him."

"Nor has anybody. He's handled by Morris Stern."

"Morrie, huh?"

"You know Mr. Stern?"

"Sure. Everybody knows Morrie. The creep."

"Then that makes it even easier. I want you to find this Bill Koeller."

"No problem."

"I need pictures, Harper."

Pause.

"Pictures, huh?"

"Straight pictures, and he's to know nothing about it. Get a good photographer onto him,

119

someone who knows how to stay out of sight. I want shots from all angles, maybe twenty. Standing, sitting, walking. Life-size blowups, in color. Handle it how you want."

"But this turkey's not to know nothing."

"Correct."

"That's all, huh?"

"That's it."

An exhaled sigh of relief. "You got it. By when?"

"I want those blowups right here, in my hands, one week from today."

"A week? Jesus, I don't think we— How'm I to—"

"One week, Harper."

"Yes, ma'am."

OCTOBER 23, FRIDAY

Chetty ran nimbly among the bushes, pursued by a sweating, furious Connie. She swung herself into the lower branches of a tree, to squat, a derisive pixie, just out of reach of Connie's grasping, pudgy hands.

"Momma Mia, Momma Mia," Chetty sang with vicious glee, "Connie's gotta diarrhea!"

"Chetty Driscoll, you'd just better get on down here."

Chetty stuck out her tongue. "Try and catch me then."

"You know I can't catch you. C'mon, now. My mom said for us to be back . . ."

"*Connie's* a fatso, *Connie's* a fatso . . ."

"If you don't get on down here right *now*. . ."

"Poo poo!"

"You lousy little shit," Connie snarled. "Just you wait. My mom's gonna *get* you. And *your* mom."

"I don't know why Connie puts up with you," Frances said later, angrily. "If you're so mean and rude, she's not going to want to take you out."

"Good," said Chetty. "She's dumb and fat, and mean, and I hate her." Chetty had never before felt so lonely and abandoned. "When's Daddy coming home, Mommy?"

"In about three weeks."

"Three *weeks*." To Chetty, it might as well have been years. And Liam never came any more. She called and called him, but he never answered. She wanted to tell him her mother was sick or something. She lay around a lot and never did anything.

"I *hate* that Connie," Chetty said again, kicking angrily at the rug.

"Oh darling," Frances said, "I wish you'd try and like her. She's really nice to you," thinking: Of course she hates Connie; she's dreadful. What's the *matter* with me? Then, "Listen, maybe I'll be O.K. tomorrow. We'll go out somewhere and have fun."

Chetty's eyes sparkled. "Can we go to Sausalito?"

"No," said Frances sharply. "Not Sausalito. I'll take you to the Children's Zoo."

"I don't want to go to the Children's Zoo. I went there with Connie *three times*, even."

"O.K. then, we'll go someplace else. Let's

feed the ducks at the Civic Center. Would you like to do that?"

Chetty shook her head. "I want to see Uncle Liam."

"Darling, I'm sorry. Not tomorrow."

"Why not tomorrow?"

"Just because."

"But I haven't seen Uncle Liam in *ever* so long."

"He'll be dropping by soon, and you'll see him then."

"I want to see him *tomorrow*."

"No."

Chetty's eyes blazed. Her face worked and she stamped her foot. "I hate you!" she screamed, her voice ugly and raw. "I hate you, Mom. *Why* can't I see Liam? He's the only person I love, and you don't let me see him. I hate you, and I hate Daddy—" Chetty stamped her foot hard on the floor, an unsatisfactory stamp into the thick rug. She picked up the nearest weapon she could find, a porcelain vase which Frances no longer had the energy to fill with flowers, and flung it at her mother. It missed, but struck the wall behind her, shattering to fragments on the floor.

"Oh *God*," whispered Frances. "Oh, Chetty darling."

Chetty's face drooped and she began to cry with tired, dragging sobs. Frances held out her arms but Chetty would not go to her. "I just want Liam. I call him and call him, and he doesn't answer. He doesn't love me any more either."

"Chetty," said Frances sharply, "how do you call him?"

But Chetty just cried louder.

"Well, hi there," said the short, well-dressed stranger. "Heard you weren't feeling too chipper, and called in to check on you."

Frances said, rather limply: "I don't believe we've met."

"We haven't met, no indeed," twinkled the little man, "but my wife has talked a lot about you. I'm Gordy Spriggs."

"Oh," said Frances. "Oh, yes." Dr. Spriggs. Of course.

He tucked his head to one side, looking at her, and said, businesslike: "Heard from Eleanor and the girls that you hadn't been feeling up to things. Can't have that. No sir, can't have that. Not with your husband gone, and everything. Know how you feel; thought I could help."

"That's nice of you, but I don't know. I don't suppose there's much anyone can do." Then, fearing she had sounded rude, she added quickly: "It really is very nice of you to stop by. Won't you come in?" She stood aside for him to enter her disordered house. "I've been feeling very tired lately. Eleanor's right. I'm afraid I haven't felt like doing too much housework around here. You'll have to excuse—"

"Don't even think of it," exclaimed the doctor cheerfully. "You mustn't wear yourself out. Get people to help. Have some woman come in and clean. And who is this lovely young lady?"

123

Chetty stood on the stairs, a sullen waif, face heavy with brooding suspicion. "I'm not a young lady."

"This is Chetty, my daughter. Darling, say hello to Dr. Spriggs."

"Hello Dr. Spriggs." It sounded insulting.

"I've come to fix up your mom as good as new. So she'll be pretty as you again."

"No you haven't," Chetty said balefully, eyes fixed and huge. "Mom, I don't want that man in here."

"Chetty—"

"I want him to go away."

"Well, now, young woman—"

"Don't call me that. I'm not a young woman. I'm a kid." ("He was crawly," she told Liam later. "Crawly inside. I hated him.")

"Chetty," Frances said crossly (what was wrong with the child these days?), *"Star Trek's* on. Go and watch, and stay in there until I say you can come out again. You're being very rude to Dr. Spriggs."

Chetty flounced into the playroom and slammed the door behind her. Frances turned to the doctor.

"I'm sorry. You'll have to excuse her. I'm afraid with me not feeling up to things, and my husband away, it's not very nice for her. She's lonely, you know, and bored, and I'm not doing nearly as much with her as I should. It's really my fault; usually she's such a sweet girl, even though I speak as a mother." Frances smiled winningly, and Dr. Spriggs smiled back.

"Don't give it a thought, Mrs. Driscoll. I know kids."

"That's very understanding of you, Dr. Spriggs."

"Gordy."

"Gordy. Did you want to examine me, then, or something?" For the first time Frances noticed he carried a black doctor's bag in his left hand. "Shouldn't I come to the office, though? I mean, I don't want to impose—"

"No problem," said the doctor, "I was passing. May as well save you the trip." He fastened a blood pressure cuff around her upper arm. "Now then, let's just see what we have. Ah. A*ha*."

"Low, huh?" said Frances.

"In good time," said Gordon Spriggs, "all in good time." He listened to her heart. Tapped her about the back while she said "Ah." Peered into her throat. "Feeling tired, my dear? Kind of pulled down? Everything too much trouble?"

"Probably the move—"

"Now, come on. A fine young girl like you shouldn't get wiped out just by a move. No, my dear. It happens to us all. Especially to you women. Sometimes, just as granny used to say, we get run down. I'll bet you're not sleeping properly, either." Dr. Spriggs burrowed in his bag. "And you're right, your blood pressure's on the low side. Perfectly normal, but a little low. Now then, where—ah, here we are. I happen to have here a guaranteed perker-upper." He handed a small green bottle to Frances.

"What is it?"

"Vitamins," said Dr. Spriggs. "Multiple vitamins and iron. Just what's needed. Tonight, when you go to sleep, take four."

Frances repeated foolishly: "At night? When I go to bed? Four?"

"Time-release spansules," twinkled Dr.

Spriggs. Come morning, you'll wake up fresh as a daisy. And you don't have to pay me, it's a sample. Don't forget them, now. You'll be surprised how they'll pick you up. Couple of days and you won't know yourself."

He stood up, straightening his jacket across his tight little paunch. "Just you take care, now. Everything's going to be peachy dandy."

"Dr. Spriggs, I don't know how to thank you."

"Rubbish, my dear. Anything to help out. That's what neighbors are for, to help out. You want to thank me, don't forget your pills."

"I won't forget," said Frances. "And thanks again. Say 'hi' to Eleanor . . ."

SUNDAY MORNING, OCTOBER 25, 2:00 a.m.

She had taken her first dose of Gordon Spriggs' vitamins, and felt almost immediately a beautiful heat in her belly which spread outward through her body in concentric ripples to culminate in a pulsing tingle in her fingers and toes. Frances lay spread-eagled on the bed, fully knowing her extremities for the first time in her life, half-formed images crowding into her head, one upon the other, faster and faster, so that soon it seemed her mind was a densely packed railroad station, the thoughts pushing and jostling one another like commuters rushing for their trains, hurrying, gone before they were clearly recognized, while new ones arrived on their heels to be crowded out in their turn.

It was enjoyable to lie like that, staring through half-opened eyes at the low, bulging moon, enormous and crimson behind the East Bay hills, not knowing whether she slept or was awake. The dreams merged into wakefulness and back into dreams like the gentle waves made by a barograph in fair weather. Liam sat at the end of her bed drinking from a can of Olympia beer. Although she knew the room to be dark, she could see every feature of his face clearly, which was strange although at the time quite natural. He looked straight toward her, his face very young and rather fretful. "Oh crap," Liam said, "I blew it." "But why?" Frances asked, puzzled. "You mustn't think that because you . . ." and like a reel of film with sequences reversed, she lay with Liam, naked on the best Bokhara. (Had it really happened, then, with Liam, after all?) He was hard and knowing, his hands cruel, and she struggled against him and loved it. And then she stood by the marble mantel, biting her knuckles watching the back of his car turn the corner past the Bombolini's driveway. An endless, flashing montage of images. Liam walking with Chetty. Liam playing hearts with Florence. Washing down the Chrysler with a hose at Waldo Point. Lying in the sun on the deck of the houseboat. Sitting across the table from her at *El Sombrero*, drinking Carta Blanca beer. Liam looking earnest, sitting on the sofa in the San Francisco flat. Sulky at a family supper. At the church for Chetty's baptism, impatient and bored. A waif-like adolescent on Valencia Street, with oversized hands and feet, glaring freckles and a bad cough. At fourteen, her first sight of him, thin face wrenched with pain, red hair wild, erupting into his mother's kitchen—"Please, Ma, I *gotta* talk with you"—and on seeing Frances, an instant's poised suspension before whirling, banging out through the front door, and bounding away down the street, his young, narrow backview, in too-short blue jeans and sneakers with his toes out, running, frantic, and Mrs. Driscoll calling, "Liam! Come back, Liam. Come on back here—please, Liam, come back!" Diminishing. Smaller. Gone.

Knowing she was awake, Frances gazed at the moon, which had moved up from the hills and hung, contracted and brilliantly white, over the Bay.

"Mom," said Chetty, "Mom, I'm frightened. Mom?" In the cold light Frances could see her bedroom door without having to move her head, which was far too heavy to lift. "Mom," Chetty said again, "I'm frightened. Grover's breaking things downstairs. Mommy? Please wake up."

The moon had moved once again, to shine from further up the window. Patterns of light shifted about her to group themselves into a different face. It was not Liam's face or Chetty's—had Chetty really been here? This was a stranger; she was certain he was a stranger. If I'd seen that man before, dreamed Frances, I'd remember, for he was, by ludicrous coincidence, a composite of her perfect fantasy lover. His pale hair hung thick about his ears; his unwinking eyes glinted green. His mouth was wide and sensitive, the lips drawn down at the corners.

He was far too real to be a dream.

She could reach out her hand and touch his face. He was *there*, complete, to the pores of his skin and the tiny fine hairs in his nostrils. No, decided Frances, he's no dream.

Chetty woke up at three o'clock, which was when Grover began to howl. For several minutes she lay listening to him. His voice rose piteously in the kitchen, wavered, dropped. She heard a crash of breaking glass, and the metallic sound of his sharp puppy nails clawing fruitlessly at the door. Chetty's heart contracted in fright. She huddled in the bedclothes waiting for her mother to hear, to turn on the lights, to go downstairs to reassure and scold Grover, but Frances made no move. "Oh, Mom!" said Chetty in disgust. She crawled from her warm bed, found her slippers and robe, and went to wake Frances. Grover yelped and tore at something downstairs. Chetty heard a crash of crockery, but still Frances slept although her eyes were half open; Chetty could see a minute white gleam from under each eyelid. She stood looking down at her mother, biting her lip, wondering what to do, then bravely left the moonlit master bedroom, with the huge bed in which Frances lay dreaming of Warren Pitt, and turned on the landing light.

From below, Grover's voice had sunk to an agonized whine. He must be hurt, thought Chetty, gaining courage, and she ran to him. Grover cowered in the kitchen, among the remains of Frances' supper dishes, which she had not put into the dishwasher the night before. His newspapers lay scattered and ripped, tossed frantically about the floor. His water bowl was overturned, and his food dish kicked under the table in the breakfast nook.

"Oh, Grover," said Chetty reprovingly, "Oh, bad," then stumbled as he caromed between her legs to fetch up breathlessly at the front door.

"You want out?" Chetty asked politely. She could open the door easily; the heavy bolts at the top were undone. Frances never bothered to lock up properly any more. She pulled the heavy door open toward her and Grover was out. She could see him plainly, his pale coat glinting in the moonlight, galloping down the driveway, to disappear into Woodburn Lane.

"Oh, Grover," sighed Chetty. The night was warmer than she had thought, and the moonlight so bright she was able to see almost as well as by day. She took his leash from where it hung beside the door, and followed.

It was 3:00 A.M., and Marta Moore had to go home to her husband. She swung lithe, naked legs to the floor, and sat up. Her lover lay beside her, out cold. Marta traced a titillating line with a beautifully lacquered fingertip down through his gold chest hair, toyed with his navel, and scratched his stomach gently. He did not stir.

"Bill," said Marta softly, "it's past three. I have to go. You said you'd take me home." As usual he was out as dead as a carcass hanging on a hook in a meat truck. Marta sighed. She would take a shower as usual, and the sound of the running water would wake him.

But even after the shower, Bill Koeller lay inert, "as though he'd died and somebody'd

stuffed him," Marta said with irritation. She
had to leave or her husband would be home
from the club where he tended bar, and so far
she had been so clever . . . Marta made one
last effort and shook Bill's shoulder hard. His
flesh felt cool and clammy. She moved his head,
which flopped back again into position, heavy
and loose. She pulled back his eyelids—"Hey,
Bill, are you there?" And could see no iris. His
eyeballs had rolled back in their sockets, which
frightened Marta, but when she reached for
his wrist, the pulse beat was steady and reassuringly strong.

Marta Moore said "Shit." She dressed
quickly. Bill's wallet lay on his dresser. She
looked through it, found two fives and a
twenty. She took the twenty for cab fare.

SUNDAY MORNING, OCTOBER 25, 9:00 a.m.

Frances sat hunched over her morning coffee
in a very bad mood. She had woken, after ten
hours of fitful, forgotten dreams, feeling sour
and depressed, more so than usual despite Gordon Spriggs' vitamins. At first she remembered
she felt marvelous. But now—what a letdown!
Perhaps it took a day or two for her body to
get adjusted. She'd give it a chance; call him
Tuesday if she still felt like this. She glowered
around the kitchen, which was a wreck. Grover
was gone—for some reason which was not sat-
isfactorily explained, Chetty had let him out in
the middle of the night, chased him half-way

across the county, and returned wet and muddy. And so, of course, this morning she had a cold. She sniffled until Frances thought she would scream: "Chetty, will you *please* blow your nose."

"I don't have a hankie."

"Then use a paper towel. Or a paper napkin."

"There aren't any."

I suppose not, thought Frances wearily. I'll *have* to get out and go shopping. She leaned her tired head in her hands, while Chetty, cheerful despite her cold, began to fill her in on the night's adventures.

"Mrs. Van Raalte's house—sniff—was all lit up, not with electric—sniff—lights, I don't think. It sort of flickered. I think it was sniff—candles, even. And there was music and singing and shouting. Sniff."

"She's too old to give parties like that," said Frances, who longed to return to bed with her coffee and drowse and read for the whole morning.

"I could see Mrs. Bombolini through the drapes," continued Chetty cheerfully. "She didn't have any clothes on—sniff—and she was dancing around."

Frances looked at Chetty coldly. "You were dreaming."

"I was not."

"Chetty, I will not listen to lies about Mrs. Bombolini."

"Mommy—sniff—I am not telling lies." Chetty added defiantly: "Connie was there too, and she didn't have any clothes on either. Yeccch."

Frances struggled to imagine the appalling

reality of Gina Bombolini without her clothes. Could Chetty be telling the truth, and Mrs. Van Raalte gave Saturday Night Swingers' Parties? Surely not. No, rationalized Frances, it had been very late, Chetty was confused, out at night by herself, had returned to bed and dreamed the whole thing. It was impossible that Gina and Connie Bombolini would be dancing—*dancing naked!* Her mind recoiled— in Mrs. Van Raalte's house, whom they apparently barely even knew, at three A.M.? Naturally, to Chetty, some dreams were extraordinarily vivid. She would not have the experience to distinguish the dream from reality under such circumstances; it must have seemed real enough. Even she herself had had some weird dreams the night before—but to think of Gina and Connie Bombolini of all people!

"And Mr. Bombolini," added Chetty casually.

Frances stared at her. "Mr. Bombolini, huh."

"Sure," Chetty said with gusto. "He's gross."

Frances could believe her.

"And I saw his wienie"—sniff.

"Chetty," said Frances forcefully, "that's enough. I don't want to hear any more."

"But Mom—"

"I'm sure you think you're telling the truth, darling," said Frances, "but I think it was a dream—just a very very clear dream," she added earnestly.

"It was not either a dream," said Chetty angrily.

And with a flash of inspiration—it's the man in the park, thought Frances, anguished. Of course, it has to be the man in the park. She's having nightmares. It's been the man in the park all along, and I never thought she'd been frightened.

So she spoke tenderly to Chetty, who had not been at all alarmed by the man in the park, or by her glimpse of the Bombolinis, and all the other people, dancing in the nude. Chetty swung her feet impatiently, knowing what she had seen, not understanding why her mother made such a big deal out of that, when Grover was lost. She did not seem at *all* worried about Grover.

Oh, Liam, yearned Chetty, you'd believe me. I could tell *you* about it, you'd know I wasn't telling lies. And you'd find Grover for me too. Suddenly miserable, she scuffed the sole of her shoe against the chair leg. Liam hadn't been to visit for what seemed years. Perhaps he didn't love her any more. What had she done to make him stop loving her? To her immense dismay, Chetty began to cry, and Frances comforted her for all the wrong reasons.

SUNDAY NIGHT, OCTOBER 25, 8:30 p.m.

"Just stopped by, dear, to see how you were getting along." Gina Bombolini settled herself comfortably into the strongest chair, accepted the drink Frances offered—"Thanks, dear, bourbon's fine"—and presented a small, cloth-covered basket. "I did some baking, dear. Had this wild urge to bake cookies. Ought to know better, shouldn't I?" Gina laughed and her jowls swung. "Try one. They're good. I've been eating them all afternoon."

"Gina, that's nice of you. Thanks. Chetty will be so excited—we're all out of cookies."

"Try one."

"I will." Frances looked into the basket.

"See, I put them into this nice little basket—make'em look more gifty. You can keep it. Use it for putting plants in, or something."

"That's nice," Frances said again. "Thanks." The cookies were tempting. Suddenly she felt hungry, remembered she had forgotten her own lunch, and after Chetty had gone to bed she had not felt interested enough to fix any supper.

Frances felt the saliva in her mouth. Suddenly, she was ravenous and Gina the kindest, most thoughtful of neighbors.

She smiled at Gina, who smiled back expectantly, and bit into the deliciously crisp, sugared cookie, which melted on her tongue.

"Glad you like them," Gina said, reaching into her needlepoint bag for her canvas and silks. "There's nothing like a cookie, dear, when you've been feeling a bit low."

"They're gorgeous," said Frances, taking a second. "I'll have to hold back, or there'll be none left for Chetty tomorrow. She'll go wild about them."

"I'll bake some more for Chetty tomorrow," said Gina. "These are just for you. I been worrying about you—all alone, not feeling too great, not cooking proper meals, maybe. There's lots of good things in those, dear, real healthy stuff. Honey, and all that."

"You're terrific," said Frances. "You know? Here. Have one."

"No thanks," Gina said surprisingly. "I been eating them all day. There comes a time when even I've had enough."

"I suppose," said Frances, suddenly fiercely glad she would not have to share. "They're just great, Gina. Honestly. You're a fantastic cook. What's that you're making?"

"Seat covers." Gina held up her canvas. An elementary floral design, the colors somewhat garish. "I'm doing six, for the dining room chairs."

"Nice," Frances said untruthfully. "I like it."

"Well, you know what they say: 'Idle hands are the devil's tools.'" Gina giggled. "I do this, and I don't bake. I like doing things with my hands. And sitting down. And you can always take it around with you."

"That's great," said Frances, and shook her head, blinking, as the room swayed and tilted.

Gina asked: "And how's Chetty? Connie does *love* taking care of her."

"She's fine, I suppose," said Frances. "She has a cold. She was worried about Grover—he got out last night, and she had to go chasing him all over the countryside."

"He came back all right, I see," said Gina.

"Oh, sure, he was back this morning." Frances gazed with exasperation at the comfortably curled puppy at her feet. "Scratching at the door and yelling for food. I'll swear he never stops eating."

"He's a sweet thing," Gina acknowledged, "but I've never been a dog person myself. Cats are O.K. I'll take cats any time. You can go out and leave them and they don't tear the

136

place up. They don't mess. Yeah, I'll stick with cats."

"Nobody seems to have pets up here except us. I noticed that," said Frances.

"No," said Gina, from a million miles away.

And the cigarette pack, clearly visible on the coffee table, was not quite there. Frances' fingers closed on emptiness. She reached tentatively several inches in different directions before touching the familiar, smooth, squarish shape, and then it was hard to extract a cigarette. She found it nearly impossible to align her eye, her brain and her fingers for the performance of the simplest motions. But then, as though at the turn of a switch, coordination returned, she lit her cigarette without trouble, and replied easily to Gina's question about Grover's escapade.

"Yes, Gina, you wouldn't believe—running about the county in her robe and slippers—at least she had that much sense, putting them on—No wonder she caught cold." Frances gazed hypnotically at Gina's needlepoint, at the dismal floral pattern now suddenly exotic and beautiful, at the vibrant, exciting colors. "Goodness, Gina," exclaimed Frances, tripping over the words with her dry, suddenly enlarged tongue, "I *love* what it is that you're making."

Gina looked at her. "Feeling O.K., dear?"

Frances swallowed. "Sure. I'm fine. I'd better not have another drink; I remembered I haven't eaten all day."

"Sure, dear. It catches up on you. Maybe I better go if you're not feeling too good."

"Oh, no, Gina, I feel fine." Frances half rose in dismay. "Please don't go," she begged, as Gina showed signs of putting away her beautiful work in its bag, surely, herself, one of the most kindly, marvelous people in the world. "Hey," Frances said, with a high-pitched giggle, "Guess what? Something to tell you. Chetty dreamed about you last night. Guess what she said?"

"What did Chetty say?" asked Gina.

"You'll never believe." Frances dissolved into helpless, hysterical laughter. "She swears it wasn't a dream. Can you imagine? She—she—chased Grover up to Mrs. Van Raalte's house—" She didn't see Gina suddenly stiffen, for she was laughing much too hard and Gina was on the other side of a rippling curtain and her edges were much too blurred—"and looked in the window. And guess what."

"Tell me, Fran."

"She saw you, and Connie, and—and—" Frances struggled and gulped while the tears ran down her face. "M—M—Mister Bombolini, dancing around, naked as jay-birds!"

"She *didn't!*" Gina's fat face creased into delighted folds and her huge body shook. "Jeez, that kid. Can you imagine! Me!" She threw back her head and laughed luxuriously.

"I told her it was because—uh—" Frances groped her way through a mind which was unfamiliar, an unknown house populated with strangers, for the thoughts and memories which she knew were hidden there somewhere. Dimly she wanted to tell Gina Bombolini, this kind, understanding person, about her anxiety, about Chetty's experience in the park, but a vital link was lost somehow between the thoughts and the words. She couldn't *say* it. She stared at Gina, her fists crammed to her mouth to stifle the tearing laughter, while with one elbow she knocked her drink to the floor. It lay there, ice cubes and liquor spilled on the rug.

Grover twitched in his sleep.

Gina picked up Frances' smoldering cigarette and stubbed it out.

And the doorbell rang.

"The door," Gina said, watching Frances. "Fran, there's someone at the door."

"Who can that be? It's late," said Frances. She fumbled her way across the living room into the hall, toward the front door, and the tall shadow thrown against the frosted glass panels by the porch light.

The blonde man smiled down at her, his eyes tender and knowing.

"C—come in," said Frances.

And she never heard Grover's whimpering as he crawled on his belly across the living room floor, tail flattened, leaving a thin trickle of urine behind him.

Mrs. Van Raalte lay on her bed, flat on her back, very still, wide eyes drinking in the life-size features of the yellow-haired man from the twenty-two huge color prints which jostled each other for space across each wall and the ceiling. There he was; stepping into his car. Walking. Barefooted, on the beach. Laughing. Talking. Pensive. Sullen. Vacant. In restaurants, offices, a bank, the lobby of an apartment house. Allowing the fabric of his body to merge with her brain, her bones, her skin, her blood, while:

"It's time," Gina told Connie. She sat in her plastic breakfast nook, backsides ballooning over the edges of the too-small vinyl seat, watermelon breasts resting on the table top. Connie looked up from her homework and nodded. She scratched her head, briefly examined the oily residue in the fingernail before wiping it on her sweater, and pushed her school books to one side.

Then she sat beside her mother, in heavy-browed concentration, to join her own mind's impulses with those of Gina and eleven others radiating from the houses around the neighborhood, to focus relentlessly on Frances Driscoll with the projected image of Warren Pitt.

SUNDAY, OCTOBER 25, 9:00 p.m.

Bill Koeller and Marta Moore occupied a discreet booth at the Fleur de Lys restaurant to celebrate a month of highly successful and, better yet, undetected copulation. Marta wore a new black dress; its shoestring shoulder straps held up very little behind, and even less in the front, and the short flared skirt showed off her excellent legs very well. She attracted a lot of attention, which pleased them both.

They smiled conspiratorily at each other, their ankles twined together under the table.

"Oh, honey," breathed Marta, "Oh, I *do* love you, baby."

Bill grinned at her, and lit a cigarette. The same brand as the commercial, for which he had successfully auditioned days before. Bill swelled with pleasure. Now he could afford to take Marta to places like the Fleur de Lys. He could drink French wine; he could afford to buy gas for his car. Things were working out at last, and who knows, this might be his big break. He ran his finger around inside the neck of his gray silk turtleneck, and brushed an imaginary speck of dirt from the sleeve of his Cardin jacket, newly purchased that afternoon. He knew he looked marvelous. He began his soup, which was hot, thick, and excellent. The wine waiter arrived with a bottle wrapped in a napkin; the label was displayed for Bill's gratification, the cork carefully drawn and presented, a tiny libation poured into his glass to be twirled, inhaled, sampled with closed eyes and smacking lips. "It's good," said Bill happily, "excellent. Wonderful bouquet."

"Oui, monsieur." The wine waiter rearranged the napkin and began to fill Marta's glass.

"And you can take away the iced water," said Bill.

"Certainement, monsieur."

And without warning, Bill clapped both hands to his head at the onset of a stab of excruciating pain and slumped headfirst into his onion soup. His glass of iced water rolled over, to send a trickle of freezing liquid across the table into Marta's nearly naked lap. One flaccid arm snapped the stem from his wineglass; a small expensive puddle of Nuits St. Georges soaked quickly into the white cloth to leave a round stain like blood.

"Christ," said the wine waiter, still holding the napkin-wrapped bottle. Marta screamed, and the other diners craned excitedly around the edges of the booth. With belated presence of mind the waiter put down his bottle and dragged Bill's scarlet, scalded face from the soup bowl. Marta stared into the face of her lover, at the stickily dripping soup, the croutons clinging to the soaking edges of his carefully styled hair, at the gray turtleneck and beautiful new jacket, now ruinous with steaming, garlicky grease. Bill flopped lifelessly back in the banquette, mouth hanging, eyes gleaming white slits.

"Jesus, lady," said the waiter, whose Continental accent had vanished like smoke, "he done this before? Whatsa matter with him?"

"I dunno," said Marta shortly, her first reaction one of intense irritation that Bill should have chosen so humiliating a way to be taken ill. Falling in his soup, yet, the dumb jerk. Couldn't he at least have waited until after dinner? And then terrible visions crowded into her shallow mind to replace anger with sheer panic. Ambulances; hospitals; Bill in the Emergency Room; herself explaining to the doctor; perhaps newspapers (But surely Bill wasn't that famous) and—her husband. "I gotta get out of here," she snapped, snatching for her purse (a gift from Bill) and her smart burnt orange coat, disappearing in a frantic whirl of beautiful legs between the small tables, where people stared at her, rushing for the door which was held open for her with automatic courtesy. "Hey, lady!" cried the waiter helplessly, "lady, wait!" . . . into the neon street, the safety and anonymity of the blaring traffic, the rushing people. For the second time in a week she flagged her own cab to take her home. Jesus, thought Marta, collapsed in relief on the back seat, what a crummy thing to have happen. What a bum. Makes it twice already; and tonight—Marta winced at

the intrusion of another sour little thought—
I'll have to pay for my own fucking cab.

SUNDAY, OCTOBER 25, 9:00 p.m.

Liam had returned to his haunts of Before
Florence, although the original reason for the
seeking of such havens had reversed. He was
now exactly like everyone else. Florence had
said waspishly: "When all you think about is
yourself and pleasing your own stupid cock,
what do you expect? Of course it's no use.
You're sapped. Your body's taken you over
and," Florence tapped her forehead, "you can't
function *at all* up here."

"Who cares?" said Liam.

"Oh, get out of here," snapped Florence.
"You make me sick. And don't you come back,
neither, not till you've got yourself together."

"Screw you," Liam said defiantly, certain at
first that he felt only vast relief at the change
in himself but unwillingly beginning to know
better, for however he tried to convince himself to the contrary, he had suffered a loss.
Something had gone.

In compensation, and carried wildly forward
on a surge of what could only be described as
lust, following his body's awakening with
Frances, he had fucked so many girls he had
lost count, he thought drearily. And here he
was, worse off than he had been three years before, with Florence furious and his body
drained and abused by loveless encounters,

glaring into his beer in preparation for another night of drink, cheap food (Florence
would no longer cook for him) and ferocious
and anonymous fucking. Liam shivered, feeling
suddenly ill, and, unwillingly practical, began
to think of possible unpleasant side effects of
his newly awakened and thoroughly gross sex-
uality. Of venereal disease. Of senselessly and
heedlessly impregnating some girl too stoned to
notice or even care he was inside her, like the
child now recovering from Florence's ministra-
tions on the houseboat.

"Oh, Jesus," said Liam in indescribable self-
disgust, "what am I doing?" Definitely, now,
he felt sick to his stomach, and he put his beer
down. He swallowed convulsively, his throat
dry and swollen. His head ached, and he sank
forward to rest his hot forehead in his hands,
thinking of influenza, hepatitis, viral pneumo-
nia. Christ, thought Liam, where I've been
lately, I might have picked up *anything*.

Never before had he known such a rapid onset of symptoms. He was locked, sweating, into
his chair, unable to rise. He felt terrible. And
then, through the stabbing flashes in his head
he began to see Frances' face, and to hear her
voice, distorted and faint, like a whisper in an
echo chamber. He shook his head violently, and
the image of Frances shivered like a reflection
in gently disturbed water.

She was calling out—somebody's name?
Liam strained to hear. It was some name
like—Ron? War*ren?"*

Something like that.

Crazy.

CHAPTER NINE

Monday, October 26, 11:00 A.M.

"But I *gotta* talk to you. The kid was out Saturday night, and saw in through the window. One of the shades musta rolled up—"

Mrs. Van Raalte glared at the telephone. Always something that went wrong, despite the most careful plans. That came of dealing with fools.

"What'll I *do?*" demanded Gina.

"How do you know? The mother tell you?"

She listened intently to Gina's hoarse, heavy voice, to the indignant narrative. "What'll we do?" Gina asked again.

"Nothing," said Mrs. Van Raalte. "There's nothing we can do, and anyhow, who'd *believe* a kid of five telling a story like that."

"And—" Gina's voice became a shaking squeak, "the hippy brother-in-law just turned up the driveway. What about *him?*"

Mrs. Van Raalte said: "Gina, pull yourself together at *once.* You're getting hysterical."

145

"But he'll talk to her. He'll *see* her."

"So what?" said Mrs. Van Raalte rudely. "Of course he'll see her—and no bad thing, either. She's not reached a point where she obviously can't take care of the child; to him she'll just look slovenly and disoriented and the house will be a mess. Probably just what he's used to," she added disparagingly. "And having seen her on the way down, his testimony will be a useful back-up afterwards."

"I don't understand," said Gina.

Mrs. Van Raalte sighed. "When Frances Driscoll is found dead of an overdose, wherever she is found, and her death is investigated, her brother-in-law's evidence will prove that it was not an accident, that she had been taking drugs for weeks, probably, beforehand."

"Oh," said Gina.

"So think of his arrival as a piece of luck. I should have thought of it myself," said Mrs. Van Raalte. "So now, will you please forget about what the child saw, and put the brother-in-law out of your mind. And *please* don't call again unless it's for something important."

Mrs. Van Raalte hung up wearily, wondering why she had been forced to surround herself with such a gaggle of dreary bores. Would it not have been possible to achieve as much, or even more, with people of her own type and class? But it was worth it. For just one more week would she have to endure such company, or perhaps, to be realistic, slightly longer until she was cleared of any possible involvement in the sad death of Frances Driscoll and the unaccountable disappearance of her daughter, and then she would be away, forever free, invulnerable, the world at her feet. Mrs. Van Raalte sighed voluptuously, thinking of the magnificent Dr. Feldman, with his clinic in Gstaad, and the miracles he wrought against the depredations of time and nature; where such miracles had been wrought on her body for the past thirty years. And then—and then—with her power, her money, her ageless beauty, her brain, and endless time at her disposal, she could rule the world.

So obviously it was necessary to associate with fools, for none of them guessed—not one. They really believed, these twelve, pathetic disciples, that they were working for themselves, and not just for her, and that they, too, would live forever . . .

Only Donald Shapiro had guessed, him with his cunning commercial brain; her only miscalculation. "I'd better be in on it too," he had said, "or I go to the police and I tell them. I tell them about the animals, I tell them everything." And she had appeared to consider, but laughed at him inside, at his brash confidence, his pleasure in his own cleverness, and above all at his pathetic vulnerability. Mr. Shapiro enjoyed his food and drink, and the salesman's lifestyle provided constant overindulgence in both. The heavy meals, combined with the long, sedentary hours in his car, crossing and recrossing northern California in air-conditioned, cushioned comfort, placed a terrible strain on his over-large, hypertensive heart. It had been so easy, Donald Shapiro such a simple target, dying as he sat waiting for her, strangling in his own vomit in a paroxysm of fear so total that the diseased heart inside him had burst like a rotten orange, and then waiting three days through the heat of Indian summer to be

147

found by Rosemary, who had guessed how he had died but had never known why.

Remembering, Mrs. Van Raalte indulged herself with a delighted chuckle before composing herself once more for much-needed sleep.

MONDAY, OCTOBER 26, 11:00 a.m.

What will she say? Liam wondered fearfully. How will I handle it? He had fought his compulsion to go to Frances for fifteen hours, all through a sleepless night, but it was too strong to be denied any longer. He swung the striped car through the heavy, late morning traffic, tensely contemplating the strained artificiality there would be between them. It will be terrible, decided Liam in panic. What am I doing? I meant to wait much longer before I saw her again; until after Jack came back from Saudi Arabia.

As he swung off the freeway, onto the off ramp for San Anselmo, turned right and began his steep climb for the ridge, along the top of which ran Woodburn Hills Road, he felt again the powerful surge of heated blood through his body, and the now familiar tightening of his jeans at the crotch. He exhaled forcefully, shook himself, turned up the sharp driveway to 40 Woodburn Lane and sat for several minutes after switching off the engine, calming and controlling himself, while his stomach clutched and twisted in anguish, the blood pounded through his veins with sickening thuds, and

Gina Bombolini peered at him through her kitchen curtains.

He need not have worried. Frances smiled at him mechanically, her eyes wide and blank, and asked him routine questions. "You look tired," (not really interested); "late night, maybe?"

"Yes," Liam said daringly. "A lot since I saw you last."

Frances raised finely feathered brows, frowning slightly—not *remembering*, Liam realized. She doesn't even *remember*.

He said: "Fran, I'm sorry about what happened. I guess you know now how I feel about you, but I wouldn't have had that happen. I'm really sorry."

"Sorry?" Frances stared at him. "What? Oh, *that*. Listen, don't worry. It's quite all right, Liam. I'd forgotten all about it."

Liam said angrily: *"Forgotten?"*

Frances smiled at him, quite abstracted. She had spent the morning lying on her bed reliving the previous night with Warren. She had stood before the mirror naked, tracing with self-satisfaction the livid claw marks on her breasts and thighs, rubbing her fingers between her legs, where the soft labial tissues were pulped and swollen, licking at her bitten lips with fierce pleasure. And he would come again *tonight*. Her belly gave one tremendous throb of expectation, and the room darkened and swam around her. Her eyes closed while the color drained from her face.

Liam asked anxiously, "Are you all right, Fran?"

Frances smiled at him slyly. "Yes, thanks, Liam. Quite O.K." Bruised and battered,

149

maybe; but quite, quite O.K., the survivor of a night so incredible that sex with Jack now seemed quite remote and tepid. She looked back with dismissal across eight years of what she had so mistakenly believed to be a satisfactory, and at times even exciting, relationship. And now here was Jack's little brother come to call, to say he was sorry he had kissed her. *Kissed* her! But it seemed to matter to him, so she tried to be polite.

Liam was speaking. "Hey," he said, "who's this?"

"Who's— Oh. Oh yes. That's Grover."

"Is he yours?" Liam bent to scratch the soft fur around the puppy's ears. "I didn't know you'd got a dog."

"Jack got him. For protection." Frances yawned. "Didn't you know about Grover?"

"How should I?" Liam said gently.

Frances said nothing, and the puppy leaned against Liam's leg, pressing with a quiet desperation.

"Something wrong with him?" asked Liam.

Frances shrugged. "How should I know? I hadn't noticed anything. I don't know much about dogs."

Liam lifted Grover into his lap. Frances stared moodily down at the dirty rug. There was a pause, until Liam asked: "Where's Chetty?"

"In school. It's Monday, isn't it?"

"How is she?"

"Fine."

"That's good."

"No—er—repercussions after that accident?" (Why think of *that*, now?)

"Accident?"

"Flo and I read about it. One of your neighbors hitting a water truck right in front of the school bus—(". . . *and Rosemary Shapiro. She drinks.*") Was it Chetty's bus?"

"Bus?" said Frances peevishly. "What bus? There was an accident?"

"You must remember," said Liam. "It wasn't more than a couple of weeks ago. It was a woman who lives—lived—around here. Someone you know. You told me about her once."

"Oh yes," said Frances. "Yes of course. Her."

"Rosemary something? Who drank?"

"Uh—Rosemary Shapiro. Yes, Chetty was there." In her foggy mind, something uncomfortable stirred. It was impossible to look away from Liam's eyes; mottled like flawed amber, they had become oddly compelling.

"Tell me about the accident," Liam said softly. "Tell me what happened with Rosemary Shapiro."

Frances said stupidly: "You read about it?"

"It was in the *Journal.* Flo reads it. It bothered me. I don't know why; I mean, it was sad and all, but there was something about it—"

"I don't know any more than what was in the paper," Frances said shortly. "Chetty did see it all, yes, but please don't ask her about it. It's all over. I don't want her having to remember. Rosemary was drunk, obviously. She didn't sound that drunk, but she must have been. Must have been bombed, poor thing. Anyway, she's dead now and it's all over. Better forgotten."

Liam said cautiously: "She didn't sound that drunk?"

"Not so bad as usual, but it was still quite early—Oh, I don't know."

"You mean you talked with her?"

"Talked? Right before. She called."

"On the phone? She called *you?*"

"Yes she did," Frances said impatiently. "Why should I call her? I barely know—knew her."

"Why did she call?"

"Oh my God, I don't know. She wanted to come over. Really, Liam, what's the point of going over it again? I don't want to talk about it. The police were quite satisfied that she was just drunk. I think there was an autopsy. Anyway, it's over now." Frances began to pace up and down the room. "Listen, Liam, I'd ask you to stay to lunch, but I don't have one thing in the house." She laughed nervously. "I must get out and go to the store this afternoon. And I was just starting on some housework. I wish I'd known you were coming and I'd have picked up a bit around here. With Jack away I'm getting sloppy."

"That's O.K.," said Liam, thinking that sloppy was too mild a description. The pretty room even smelled bad . . . (*"It smells bad, like Mom didn't put the garbage out . . ."* Oh, Christ, Chetty said that. Right away, soon as she came in the front door. If only I'd paid some attention then, instead of getting into that mess with Fran. Have I been *blind,* wondered Liam, noticing the dusty floors, the film of ash over the bleached bricks of the fireplace, the crooked pictures, and the pot of dead, smelly chrysanthemums in Frances' prized giant antique brass planter. Is there something wrong with this house after all? And I never picked up on it?). Stubbornly he continued: "When Rosemary called, did she sound upset?"

"How should I know?" snapped Frances. "I'm telling you, she sounded just like herself. Normal, if you call that normal."

Liam sighed. "I mean, was she rambling? Or excited?"

Frances said sharply: "Must I go through it all again? No, she wasn't rambling. Actually, she was very abrupt and quite lucid, for Rosemary. Wanted to see me right away to tell me something. She said to come over to her house, but I wasn't dressed and so she said she'd come over to see me. Frankly," Frances shrugged, "she must have been bombed. What could have been that important? It was one of those sad things that happen. Gina said it was probably an unconscious death wish. Poor Rosemary was a very unhappy person. And she must have had a few drinks already, said she'd be right over, and hung up on me when I told her no, and then never showed up. I was thinking she'd just had one more and forgotten all about it, but then I heard the sirens, and the policeman brought Chetty home . . ." She walked toward the liquor closet. "Which reminds me, I think I'll have a drink. It's just bourbon now—we seem to be out of everything else. Want one?"

"All right," said Liam.

"Poor Rosemary," said Frances again on her way to the kitchen for ice and water. "It was a horrible thing to happen. Dreadful accident."

And as she left the room, Chetty spoke matter of factly from the front door: "It wasn't an accident."

Liam spun around.

"So I called and called you," she glared at

Liam accusingly, "and you never came or anything. Why didn't you come?"

"Oh Chetty," Liam said with distress, "it's not something I can explain; but it wasn't because I didn't want to. You must believe me." And then, "How do you know it wasn't an accident?"

"I just know."

"Chetty. Tell me."

"Why?" She would pay Liam back for his neglect now.

"Please. I need to know. It's maybe important."

Chetty ignored him. She bent to greet Grover. "Hello, Grover. Hello, Puppy. Are you glad to see me? Is anyone glad to see me?" Then raised her head to stare at Liam from under fiercely lowered brows. "Why's it important? Why should I tell *you* anything?"

"You don't have to," Liam agreed humbly, "but Mrs. Shapiro's accident may have something to do with your mommy." He was trying with all of his shredded power to try to reach Chetty, to offer his love, his sorrow at his neglect, and his reassurance, but for the first time in his life he was meeting a smooth, glassy wall of defense. Their eyes locked.

But then Chetty's lower lip trembled. She said: "It'll help mommy if I tell you?"

"I don't know. Perhaps."

She sighed with relief at being able at last to tell something no one but Liam could understand. "Well, O.K. then. I saw the car coming down the driveway, down Mrs. Shapiro's driveway. We could all see it, and the big truck, too—and I could feel it."

"Feel it? Feel what?"

"Just feel it. I don't know." Chetty faltered, confused. "It was kind of—like something *strong* was there."

"Something strong?"

"Yeah. Just this feeling."

"And what happened after Mrs. Shapiro crashed into the truck?"

Chetty shrugged. "It went."

Liam sat quite still and looked at her. "Now, listen very carefully, Chetty. Do you think— could it have been—I mean, that feeling, did it have anything to do with Mrs. Shapiro driving into the truck?"

"Sure," said Chetty, looking at him as though he was stupid. "It made her do it."

A chill touched the back of Liam's neck.

"O.K., it made her do it. Now listen, Chetty. When you felt there was something there, did you try and stop it? Did you do *anything*? You know what I mean."

"No," said Chetty. "It was *real* strong. Maybe even as strong as me. It was scary."

"Good," Liam said briskly, unutterably relieved. "Now listen. Have you told this to anybody else? Did you tell the policeman?"

"No. Nobody would've believed me except you. That's why I'm so unhappy when you go away. Nobody believes me, or understands me, or *listens* to me—" Chetty's voice trailed. She gulped and sniffed.

Liam gathered her into his arms. "I know, darling. And I'm sorry. I'll never go away from you again, not for that long. I promise."

"Good," said Chetty, "because I wasn't happy. I missed you. And—and—" in a final wail of anguish, "you hadn't even seen *Grover*."

155

"Right," said Liam. "It's a deal. But listen, now. I don't want you telling anybody else about Mrs. Shapiro. It's just something for me and Flo to know about. Nobody else, especially not your mom. Not right now."

"O.K.," said Chetty. Then: "Liam, *what's wrong with my mom?*"

"I don't know," said Liam. "I wish I did. How long has she been like this?"

Chetty frowned. "I'm not sure. It sort of started, then it turned a little worse after Daddy went away, and real bad after Mrs. Shapiro got killed."

"That's the sort of thing I need to know," said Liam, "to ask Flo about. Now, don't you worry. She's going to be all right."

"She is?"

"Sure she is."

"I suppose," said Chetty, unconvinced, then asked abruptly: "Liam, do you know a person called Warren Pitt?"

The name had an oddly familiar ring to it. "I'm not sure. Why?"

"Mom does."

"Warren Pitt. What a queer kind of—sort of—*underground* name. Who is he?"

"I don't know, but I heard Mom—she woke me up, Liam, she was shouting so loud. And she kept saying *Warren*—I heard her." Chetty shivered. "I wanted to ask her, but I was *frightened*, Liam. And then more times. She was kind of laughing and crying both at the same time. It sounded funny."

Liam took both of her hands in his. "Maybe she was just having a bad dream. Now, listen to me—"

"Chetty darling," said Frances, returning

156

with bourbon and water for Liam and herself, already well fortified with cookies, "back already?"

"It's twelve o'clock," said Liam. "Past twelve."

"As late as that," Frances said wonderingly, pleased to have traveled further through her meaningless day than she had believed. There was now just the afternoon to get through. She would make lunch for Chetty and pack her over to Connie's to watch television and take a nap to refresh herself for the long evening ahead. Maybe she should wash her hair. Her scalp itched. Then, later, put Chetty to bed. Take her vitamin pills—maybe a double dose. They still didn't seem to be working too well. Have a cocktail perhaps, which helped too, and then Warren would come. She ticked off the hours in her mind. Eight hours. It would seem like a year, but she would have to wait; the time would pass somehow. Until eight-thirty, when Warren would come.

"Well, look what just dragged in."

"Flo, I need to talk to you."

Florence looked skeptical.

Liam said: "I went over to see Fran."

"To see Fran. Yeah, I guess it's been a while. What about it?"

"Flo, something's *wrong* up there."

"Like what?"

Liam said, bewildered, "I don't know. But Fran's just—not herself. She doesn't seem *sick*, exactly, but she's acting real odd, and kind of gone to pieces. I mean, she looks like she hasn't taken a bath in a week. The house is dirty too—Christ, it's *filthy*. Fran would never let the place get like that. And she's not taking care of Chetty properly either. There's nothing to eat in the place."

"It's Monday. Maybe she had a rough weekend."

"It'd take a whole lot more than one weekend to make the place look like that. I'm *telling* you." He added: "It's just not *Frances*, Flo. She's one of the most alive, most balanced, beautiful people I know. I *love* her, Flo."

"I know," Florence said shortly.

"I mean, all this, what I've been into the past couple of weeks, was because I . . . I don't know how to say it, Flo."

"You should have known better," said Florence.

"I know. She's Jack's wife—"

"Jack's wife nothing. She's not for you, and you know it."

Liam looked up sharply, but Florence would not meet his eyes. After several seconds of silence he stared down at his shoes. "I know, Flo. You don't have to tell me." His voice was stricken.

"Oh, Jesus, baby, I'm sorry." For an instant, Florence reached out a meaty hand, and withdrew it. "But it would never work out. You *know* that."

"Yes. I know. It's O.K., Flo." Liam straightened his shoulders determinedly. "Got any beer?"

"Sure," said Florence gruffly, "where you'd expect. It hasn't been so long you don't remember where the goddam beer is." With reluctant tenderness she watched Liam's spare backview as he searched among the cluttered shelves of the refrigerator; at his well-muscled, hard

158

back, the narrow hips in the sagging Levi's, and the lithe, strong legs.

I did all that, thought Florence with pride. *I* took him in, such a scrawny, screwed-up kid, and it was *me* made him into what he is now. Not his mother. Not Fran. And no one can take that away from me. "If I was forty years younger," said Florence suddenly. "I looked O.K. when I was your age, Liam. I really looked like something."

"Sure you did, Flo," said Liam in surprise, who never pictured Florence to himself as ugly, fat, and old.

"Sure you did," mimicked Florence. "Oh, crap."

Liam recognized the sudden shift in mood, knew from three years' experience of Florence that the deeper her tenderness the more compensatory profanity was thought necessary, and was sensible enough to keep silent. Florence turned her back, and reached through the sleeve of her muu-muu to scratch at herself. Thinking . . . She had hoped so much to be able to protect Liam, once he had mastered his own strangeness enough to pay attention to his more ordinary human needs. She had wanted to prevent him battering himself against an alien world, as she had done, and to stop him from forming relationships, as she had done time and again, which could be at best only half relationships. But had she the right to protect him? Should she not have encouraged him to go out in the world, to find out for himself—even though he would have been hurt?

She had acted, Florence told herself, in all

good faith, with Liam's best interests at heart. She *had*.

Hadn't she?

What had she told Liam—"You should have known better." But *I* should have known better, Florence jeered to herself in a sudden unwelcome flash of brutal honesty. You crazy, interfering old fool. What were you *really* after? Didn't you really, in your heart, hope that— No wonder you were jealous of Frances, Florence snarled to herself. Admit it, you fat, dirty-minded old hooker. You were *jealous*.

"Shit," Florence said aloud, "*why* aren't I forty years younger?"

And Liam said sincerely, "I wish you were, Flo," and then with despair, "but oh, God, Flo, I wish I knew what to do about Fran."

Florence looked at him and closed her mouth like a trap.

"I mean, I feel so helpless. Something seems badly wrong with her, and I don't know what it is. Nothing's coming through. It just kills me."

"Nothing comes through at all?" Florence asked, with a slight return of professional interest.

"Well, almost nothing. Just odd pieces that don't fit. It's like trying to talk on the phone when the lines have all gotten screwed up. Nothing seems to relate, like bits of three different conversations. It's so—so ironic. The one time of my life when I really need to be like I was, and it's gone. I just can't do it. Flo," Liam asked urgently, "will it ever come back?"

"I don't know," said Florence, "but I don't see why not. Try not to worry about it. I mean, the only reason why you're different from most

160

people is being born able to recognize what you have and able to learn to control it. Everybody in the world has psychic potential. It's not magic. I read somewhere," Florence said carefully, "that magic is just the application of natural forces."

"I know," said Liam impatiently, "but—"

"So if it's a natural force, why should it stop? Why should you lose it? I guess you feel different about it now, though. It matters."

"Oh yes," said Liam. "It does. I thought it was the one thing in the world I wanted to lose, you know? I wanted to be like other people. I used to *pray*, Flo. Pray to God every night I'd wake up in the morning and be just like other people. But not now. I *can't* live without it, Flo. Not after knowing what it's like. It's like being blinded. Or—or being impotent, or something."

"I guess," said Florence. "Well, mostly with that kind of problem, tension makes it worse. Once you learn to relax it takes care of itself. Impotence, anyway."

"You think so?" he asked hopefully.

"Sure. Anyway, you never really lost it. Not if something's still coming through. You'll be O.K. It's just that everything in you was concentrated somewhere else."

Liam sighed gratefully.

"So like I said, relax and let it happen. Meantime, tell me what this is with Fran."

"Well," Liam said thoughtfully, "apart from the mess, and the dirt and all, things just seem very weird. I don't know how to describe it. I mean, Fran looked at me as though I was some kind of stranger she didn't even like much.

And then there's that Rosemary Shapiro woman. The one who got killed—remember?"

Florence nodded.

"Right before she got killed, she'd talked to Fran on the phone."

"What did she want?"

"Fran doesn't know. Rosemary didn't tell her. She was on her way over to Fran's house to see her."

Florence stared at him. "She was, huh?"

"And then Chetty said—Chetty was in the bus, you know? The school bus. They just missed the crash, and the kids saw it all."

"I remember. Go on."

"Chetty felt something. She saw Rosemary come on out of the driveway like a bat out of hell, right into the truck, and she said there was—" Liam frowned, trying to remember Chetty's exact words: *"Something strong was there."*

"She's sure? She wasn't just wanting a bit of attention, maybe? Trying to look important? Because she hadn't seen you in a while?"

"Chetty'd know better than that," Liam said indignantly. "Sure she's sure. And right after the crash, that strong feeling was gone. Chetty said she knew it had made her do it. I mean, forced Rosemary to drive into the truck."

"And Rosemary Shapiro was going to see Fran." Florence sat rock still, wearing the particularly vacant expression which Liam knew signified intense thought. After a moment, she said:

"Rosemary calling Fran and wanting to see her right away, but getting knocked off, if Chetty's right, before she gets to her, seems to me like some rather powerful person not

162

wanting Fran to know what Rosemary was going to tell her. Could Rosemary have wanted to warn Fran about something?"

"But about what?" Liam looked confused.

"Give me a beer, Liam," said Florence. "I'm thinking." With resolution, she forced her personal frustrations and suffering into the dim back storeroom of her mind where they belonged, and directed her considerable knowledge and experience toward Liam and his anxieties for Frances, drinking from the can in long gurgling drags to help her concentration. With her entire will thus focused, Florence could be very formidable.

Finally: "There's one thing," she said, "although I can't see any reason for it. Not that that means anything. We've talked about psychic attack sometimes."

"Sure."

"Basically it's no different from a curse, a hex—"

"But why should someone do that to Fran?"

"Under psychic attack, a person wilts for no apparent reason. They feel tired all the time, dragged down, sick, apathetic. Eventually they might even die. They wither away."

Liam looked shocked.

"And Jack went away—" Florence went on.

"And she doesn't see any of her old friends anymore—even before Jack went away. But Flo, why? It doesn't make any sense." Then: "It has to be something to do with the house," Liam said suddenly. "It all started after they moved in there. Somebody must want them out of the house."

Florence shook her head. "If that was all, they'd have been out long ago. They wouldn't have been able to stay there. How did the house feel to you?"

Liam shrugged. "I never picked up on anything. Not once. I always did think that was odd, looking back. Could that be—artificial? To make things look innocent when they're really not?"

"Maybe."

"They have a dog now. He's the saddest little mutt I ever saw. Just sits and shivers."

"He does?" Florence looked interested. "Then get him out of the house, and see if he changes."

"Why?"

"Even if you're picking up nothing," Florence said patiently, "the dog might be."

"O.K.," said Liam. "I'd better be getting up there pretty much every day anyway."

"Then go carefully," Florence said. "Psychic attacks are not something to be messed with. When you went up there today, did you see anybody around?"

"I'm not sure. I don't think so. Like who?"

"Like one of Fran's new neighbors?"

"Flo! You think the *neighbors*—?"

"Got any better ideas?

"But the way Fran talked about them, they all seemed so *dull*. Except for Mrs. Van Raalte, but nobody ever *sees* her."

Florence looked thoughtful. "Does Fran see anybody else these days? Other than the neighbors?"

"I guess not. She hasn't been out in weeks, and she's in no shape to go anywhere now."

"So she's stuck up there on that hilltop alone and only sees them, except for Mrs. Van Raalte. Who nobody sees. Then this Rosemary character, who wants to tell Fran something in a hurry, gets killed before she can tell it. Liam, does Fran talk about any of them in particular, would you say?"

"Only Mrs. Van Raalte."

"Mrs. Van Raalte again."

"Oh come on, Flo. You can't think Mrs. Van Raalte killed Rosemary Shapiro. She's a million years old."

"Doesn't mean anything."

"Flo, come on."

"But it does make sense," said Florence. "Mrs. Van Raalte seems to stand out from the others. And apart from everything else, she's very, very rich. She's a powerful old woman. She's very likely to be calling the shots up there. The Mrs. Van Raaltes of this world tell people to go jump," Florence snapped her fingers, "and they jump."

"Flo," Liam said, as a new thought struck him with chill force, "Jack going away like that, so unexpected, do you think that's a little too neat? Could they have fixed that?"

"It's possible."

"And Jack's away another couple of weeks. So if they had to have him out of the way for some reason, I guess—I guess something will happen to Fran before then. Flo, couldn't they come and live here until he gets back? Can't we take care of them here?"

"Sure, Liam. Just try it. The way she is now, if I'm right, she won't move from Woodburn Hills. She can't. Not even out to the store." Florence rested elbows like twin legs of lamb on the kitchen counter. "Tell you what, though. Cable Jack and have him come home. Tell him Fran's sick or something. Tell him to hurry.

They won't have any control over him now, even if they did before."

"Why not?"

"Because they can't cover all bases at once," said Florence. "And it's Fran's turn now. They're concentrating on her."

"You know the way you're talking, Flo? You make it sound so sure, all this psychic attack stuff."

"Like I said before," said Florence, "got any better ideas?" She peered across at Liam. The eyes which met hers were no longer old and wise. They were young and frightened. She knew well that Liam suspected himself in far deeper waters than he had ever believed existed, as though placed naked on a battlefield with only one weapon, and a dubious one at that.

"What am I going to do, Flo?" Liam asked.

CHAPTER TEN

Monday, October 26, 4:00 P.M.

Bill Koeller looked at himself gloomily in the mirror, at his reddened, scalded face (that French onion soup had been hot, man), and the greasy patches of ointment. He had missed his audition for the pilot; he had also had a go-see at an advertising agency scheduled for three-thirty that afternoon to be looked over by the client—men's after-shave. Oh, Jesus. At the thought of any astringent lotion touching his abused skin, an uncontrollable tremor of anguish rippled through his entire body. So he had missed out on that one, too. The whole week was shot, for it would take days for that face to settle down. He couldn't even shave—he looked terrible. Marta was gone. What in hell was wrong with him?

He had awakened in pain in the Intensive Care Unit at St. Mary's Mercy Hospital in Santa Monica. "Where the hell am I? What's *happened?*" Bill had yelled, healthily loud. His face was throbbing and angry, and his lower sheet rustled uncomfortably over the creased rubber below it, tacky and stiff with his own emissions. He must have had some pretty wild dreams, despite his agonized face. But what had happened to him? Dr. Kleinwort had suggested, "Hysterical symptoms? What else;" (Dr. Kleinwort had no sympathy for the stress of an actor's life *at all;* he simply *must* change his doctor) for there was apparently nothing wrong with him. He checked out perfectly. All blood tests within normal limits. Chest X-ray normal. EKG normal. Everything normal, notwithstanding the catheter in his bladder and the saline drip. It made no sense. To be unconscious six hours—"six *hours*," Bill repeated wonderingly—with his body functioning with full efficiency but uninhabited, so to speak. And then to wake at 3:00 A.M. in perfect health save for his ruined face, which after all, Dr. Kleinwort had told him cheerfully, was only a very temporary affliction. God*dam* Dr. Kleinwort! How could *he* know? By 3:00 P.M., even though he was supposed to be in for observation for at least twenty-four hours, Bill had had enough and determinedly discharged himself with Dr. Kleinwort's qualified consent. He must take things very easily, and report at once any deviation or change in his condition.

Bill considered. He remembered his terrible dream of the week before; it popped uncontrollably into his mind like a gas bubble. He remembered Marta calling, to tell him about the twenty she'd taken, that she'd been unable to wake him; he'd been out cold. Was there a relationship between the two episodes? Would it happen again? Was something badly wrong

with him? On some deep level, Bill had discharged himself from the hospital in case there
was. He did not feel ready to find out yet.
Something really wrong? Something untraceable and intermittent? Even though the en-
cephalograph hadn't shown anything, there
had to be a reason. He reached resolutely for
the dreaded word. Epilepsy. Bill spat the con-
sonants through his teeth like bitter fruit
seeds. What did they do for epilepsy, anyway?
How would it affect his career? How soon
would they know? When would he have another blackout? What medication would he be
on? Would he lose his driver's license? Bill now
felt afraid to go out for fear of falling in the
street. But at least there was one thing to go
on—both episodes had taken place at night.
And possibly that time when Marta had taken
the money and gone home, he could have been
just unusually heavily asleep, for as he remembered it had been a highly energetic evening.

Suppose I'm getting sick, really sick, Bill
wondered, what'll I do? How'll I pay the medical bills? The new commercial would ordinarily
add a nice shot of adrenaline to his permanently
ailing bank balance, but with heavy medical
expenses it would evaporate like a small puddle
in a desert. Perhaps this was the time to give
up the struggle for stardom, and return to his
father's brewery business in Milwaukee. Bill
poured himself a stiff Scotch, despite Dr. Kleinwort's exhortations to go easy on the liquor
too, for he felt his need was great. He was a
worried man.

TUESDAY, OCTOBER 27, 12:30 p.m.

"Something sure is the matter with Grover, Mom," Chetty said sadly. "He didn't even eat his dinner. Mom, can we take him to the doctor? He sure is sick."

Frances looked down exhaustedly at the puppy, recalling that Liam, too, had said much the same. Had it been yesterday? Monday? Everything was so hazy, and she was so tired, but Chetty was right—even she could see that something certainly was the matter with Grover. He lay in the farthest corner underneath the breakfast table, shivering and resolutely refusing to come out. "His nose is so hot and dry, Mom, and he must have a fever," Chetty said anxiously. "Please, Mom, let's get him to the doctor. To the dog's doctor," she added hopefully. His soft coat felt harsh, and by the evidence of the kitchen floor his stomach was badly upset.

"Please, Mom?"

"Maybe later. I'll—I'll try. Maybe Connie—"

Liam came later in the afternoon. For a few moments he sat perfectly still in the car, looking at the house. It could be derelict, thought Liam. There was an air of disuse and neglect. Dry leaves had blown around the front door and the area by the garbage cans was messy. He saw a banana peel, scrunched-up pieces of soiled paper, and other litter. The garden was dry and untidy.

He drove Chetty and Grover to see the vet. They had no appointment, and had to wait forty-five minutes, by the end of which Grover galloped unrestrainedly around the waiting room on his large, babyish feet, waggling his rear end, barking and snapping in such a remarkable return to high spirits that the receptionist demanded that they either control him or leave.

The vet said he was absolutely fine.

Afterwards they walked Grover down by the canal. He romped after blown leaves and garbage, and violently attacked an old glove lying in the gutter. He squatted to piddle immaturely at recognizable watering spots, and dropped a large and reassuringly normal-looking bowel movement under the censuring eyes of an old lady.

"He's O.K. now, Chetty," said Liam. "Do you think it could have been something he ate, maybe? You know how puppies are—they'll eat anything."

"I suppose," Chetty said doubtfully. "I don't think it was anything he ate, though. He's just had puppy food and milk." She added: "I wish you'd take him home with you, Liam. He just doesn't seem to like it anymore at our house. Please, Liam?"

"No, I think I'd better leave him with you," Liam said thoughtfully. "In his own way, he *is* protection."

"I took her to McDonald's for dinner," Liam said.

"Dinner?" said Frances, and began to laugh.

"Mom," Chetty said crossly, "there's nothing funny about McDonald's."

"Oh, I don't know what's funny," shrieked Frances breathlessly. "Just *everything's* funny." The expressions on Liam's and Chetty's faces were so hysterical she could barely get her breath. She fell loosely back into an armchair, weeping and shaking. "Your faces," gasped Frances. "Look at your faces!" Liam and Chetty, round pale faces with buckled features as in a sideshow at a carnival. "The mirrors," squeaked Frances, "like the funny mirrors!" They were suddenly all noses. Then eyes, noses, and mouths ran together in a curious flattened blob, and they were both all forehead, topped with tufted excrescences of hair. "Oh!" gasped Frances, holding her aching stomach. "Oh, please stop it. I can't *stand* it! So *funny!*"

"It's after six," Liam told Chetty. "Go watch *Star Trek.*"

"But Mommy—"

"I'll take care of your mom."

"But Liam—"

"Go!" And Chetty backed out of the room, confused and half frightened—first Grover, now her mom—but Liam was here, and he'd know what to do. She trailed into the playroom, obediently turned on the television she did not want to watch, and sat alone and unhappy on the sofa, her feet tucked under her, not understanding anything at all.

"All right, Fran," Liam said in the living room, "so tell me what it is you're on."

"I'm on?" Frances loosed another high-pitched whinny of laughter. "I'm not on anything."

"Don't give me that crap," said Liam. "You're stoned." He looked down at her almost in relief. If she had been taking dope all this time, it would all be so much simpler and perfectly understandable. Liam felt suddenly foolish, embarrassed for himself and Florence, half convinced now that between them they had drastically mistaken the whole affair; had endowed a few unrelated incidents with ludicrously sinister undertones, and had cooked up between them, through a misguided urge for cheap melodrama, that absurd notion of psychic attack and murderous neighbors. Apart from Rosemary Shapiro's death, which had been accepted by the police as an unfortunate, but, considering her condition, almost inevitable accident, everything else (except for Chetty's curious statement) was explained, surely, by boredom and foolishness on the part of Frances. She would have been lonely (partly his fault) stuck away up here with no one to turn to, feeling a sense of abandonment (by everyone, thought Liam guiltily), lighting up a joint perhaps in the evenings, and before long enjoying a smoke while Chetty was in school in the morning. Liam grasped gratefully at a rational explanation as eagerly as a drowning man would clutch a lifebelt.

Frances stopped giggling and looked shifty, and for a second he was able to catch her wide-eyed gaze and hold it. Her eyes were puffy and inflamed, the irises appearing much greener than usual and the pupils shrunken to dots. The evidence was plain, and Liam attempted to see through. He was partially successful. For a fleeting instant he saw Frances' mind as a series of interlocking compartments like Chinese boxes, the centermost containing a well-guarded secret which she did not wish anyone to know. But as to evidence of drug taking, he was nonplussed. According to her body, she was plainly in a drug-induced euphoria; her mind, however, knew nothing of it. Only in that innermost, well-guarded core did Liam think he would find an answer, but knew that, as surely and instinctively as he shrank from finding out, he would not, in his present state of psychic debilitation, be able to. It was a relief. He did not want to know.

"You'll have to go soon," Frances said, clearly and rationally. "I have someone coming over."

"I can't leave you like this, Fran. You're not in any shape to take care of yourself. Or of Chetty."

"But Liam—I'm fine now. Honestly, I'm O.K." She sounded quite normal. "Listen, I was tired and I had a couple of drinks earlier while you and Chetty were out. But I'm quite sober now. Don't I *look* O.K."?

"You want me to go?"

Frances nodded.

"Well," said Liam doubtfully, "O.K. then, if

you're not going to do anything dumb—" but he did not leave until he had made certain Chetty was safe in bed, Grover fed, and Frances more or less composed for her visitor. It had to be a man, Liam decided with a sudden shock of jealousy. It *had* to be. Frances was seeing someone else, and that was why she had wiped him from her mind as completely as she might wipe a dirty word off a wall. He reached for the name Chetty had mentioned. Warren Pitt. Was he the one? He dared not ask her for fear of what she might say.

Liam remained half an hour longer, lingering, while Frances became increasingly anxious for him to leave. It *was* a man, thought Liam. Oh, definitely.

On an impulse, he drove down the hill, parked in a recessed area off the road under an oak tree, and returned stealthily on foot to wait just out of sight of the house, concealed among a dense growth of fruit trees, chest-high oleander bushes and shrubbery. Although he was unable to see the house, he could see whoever came, for there was no other way to enter the driveway. Liam waited a long time. He grew very cold, felt very stupid, and once he heard Grover howl. One car drove up the hill toward him; it was a three- or four-year-old Buick, driven by an elderly man in a soft hat—Frances' lover? He turned into the Bombolini's driveway, and his swarthy face was illumined briefly as he opened the car door. It had to be Mr. Bombolini. But nobody else came, and at last Liam crept up the driveway toward number 40. The lower floor was in darkness now; the only light shone muted through the drapes in the master bedroom

175

where presumably Frances had given up waiting for her visitor and retired to bed alone. Both the Driscoll cars rested peacefully in the carport, Chetty must be sleeping. The only sound was the muted drone from the freeway at the bottom of the hill.

Liam turned, stiff and disconsolate, and left as quietly as he had come.

TUESDAY, OCTOBER 27, 9:30 p.m.

Florence stood at the old electric stove which Liam had bought for her from Goodwill Industries, absently munching a cinnamon meringue while she stirred a rich, bubbling pot of minestrone, glad to be cooking for Liam again, for he was gaunting out fast and growing pasty from the late nights, drinking, and junk food.

He should have been home long ago. Already it was past nine, but somewhere in the dark at the top of the ridge overlooking the freeway, Liam still crouched stiffly in the oleander bushes waiting in vain for Frances' lover.

Florence grated a knob of parmesan cheese into a bowl, stirred the minestrone once again and put a dish of lasagna in the oven. She rubbed the inside of the salad bowl with a clove of garlic, began to shred a lettuce, and then, with impatience, pushed everything aside, wiped off the counter, and reached below it into a small, recessed compartment, for the blue felt bag which contained her Tarot cards.

For a moment she held the deck loosely in her hands, eyes closed, waiting.

Then she chose the Page of Swords for Frances' significator, shuffled the cards and cut the deck three times with her left hand. Placing the card representing Frances firmly central with a thick forefinger and thumb, she laid out nine more cards, five to form a rough cross upon and around the significator, the other four to the right in vertical sequence.

Liam found her half an hour later, leaning on her elbows, chins resting in her hands. He looked over her shoulder, and felt his stomach turn over. "For Frances," said Liam, nodding his head helplessly.

Absently she lifted cards two and three to expose the first card for him, the reigning influence over the significator. The Queen of Swords sat stiffly on a massive gray throne backed by billowing storm clouds, staring in grim profile into unseen distance.

"A dark, older woman," Florence said unhappily. "Mrs. Van Raalte, wouldn't you say?" She turned to Liam. "I've never seen such bad cards. Never, not in my whole life."

Together they studied Florence's lay-out, which, before their eyes, seemed to mock and shimmer. There was a grinning gray skeleton wearing a black suit of armor, astride a red-eyed horse whose bridle was decorated with skulls and crossed bones. A weeping female figure, seated upright in bed below nine horizontal swords; three swords piercing a scarlet heart; and the only note of relief; a youthful male figure, gaily clothed in red and white, above whose head swam the symbol for infinity. He stood behind what looked to Liam like a redwood picnic table, upon which lay the symbols of the four suits of the Tarot: a cup, a sword, a wand, and a pentacle described on a circular ground. The card was bordered by flowers.

"The Magus," Florence said thoughtfully looking at Liam. "But his influence has gone."

Together they studied the rest. A monstrous, bloated horned devil symbolizing the subjugation of the spirit by the material and crass; the seventh card, reversed—two crippled beggars, hobbling through a heavy snowstorm. ("Disorder, chaos, and ruin," Liam whispered from memory.) The eighth card, "and the worst," Florence said with resignation: the Tower. A grey obelisk, burning against a black sky, from which tumbled two screaming figures. The ninth: a tall, scornful man who gazed after two abject fugitives. ("Degradation, destruction," murmured Liam.) But it was the tenth card which Florence studied so intently. The tenth card, the resolution, the outcome: a sturdy young man astride a prancing red horse. The Knight of Wands.

"In the end," Florence said, "she will be in the hands of this person. A blonde young man."

"Blonde," said Liam in despair. And sneezed.

"Or just as easily red-headed," said Florence, and they looked at one another. "And I hope," she added, "that I never again see cards like these." With a sweeping movement of spatulate fingers, she swept them together and replaced them into the bag. "Come, Liam," Florence said resolutely, "you're getting thin and catching cold. Eat your minestrone.

There's nothing we can do now; we'll talk more about it tomorrow."

TUESDAY, OCTOBER 27, 9:30 p.m.

"Warren," Frances gasped, turning to the man who lay beside her with the lamplight glinting on his yellow hair. "Darling, I never knew. Oh, my God, I never knew."

"Do you want it again?"

"Oh, yes. Oh, please . . ." -

"Like this?"

"Oh, yes. Harder. Please, Warren, harder."

"Like this?"

"Oh, my *God*."

There had never been a man like Warren Pitt. Never before had Frances believed a man could perform such perverse atrocities with such refined gentleness. During the day he was a furtive memory, recalled some times with a hot coiling of her belly. The nights became a seething sequence of unmentionable acts, where she became someone else, someone quite unrecognizable. Tomorrow, surely, I'll be ashamed, thought Frances each night, but the mornings found her tired and drained as usual, the events of the night before a hot, formless dream. "I'll be back," Warren had said. "Around eight-thirty. I'll see you then." And Frances had waited in unreality for eight-thirty, disposing of Liam, taking her pills, feeling, miraculously, the apathy and exhaustion drop away as the evening wore on; answering the door with ecstatic expectation; twining herself around the tall figure of Warren, who wordlessly carried her upstairs, stripped her, threw her across the big bed and gazed down on her while Frances stared up at him in an agony of helpless anticipation. And afterwards he held her aching body tenderly, licking the soft exposed inside skin of her elbow, where the artery pulsed under his fingertips, gently caressing with his tongue the whorls of her ear, and pushing back with his hand the damp, wildly tangled hair. They spoke little to each other after the initial greeting; there was not much to say.

WEDNESDAY, OCTOBER 28, 8:00 a.m.

Frances sighed with relief as Chetty trudged off down the driveway in the direction of the school bus. Her shoulders, arms and breasts ached and were crosshatched with thin red lines. Please, prayed Frances absently each night as it began, don't let Chetty hear us. But seconds later the whole world was forgotten save Warren. Now, with resolution, she took the coffee pot, rinsed it and cleaned it thoroughly with Brillo, prepared a fresh brew and plugged it in. So far, she was certain, Chetty suspected nothing; both evenings she had remembered to check before Warren arrived, and the child had been soundly sleeping. Frances wondered whether to lock her bedroom door at nights; suppose for once Chetty were to wake in the night and hear—Frances shuddered. She must be crazy; but she had to have Warren. Warren was an addiction, although how long she could physically go on, God knew. He was too much for her. He hurt her too much. And today, for the first time, she remembered everything in burning detail; Warren still lived for her, even on waking.

The coffee perked agreeably, and Frances rubbed at her gritty eyes. Warren had not left until very late; for the third evening she had finally dropped into an exhausted sleep and when she awoke, he was gone, but he would come again tonight, as soon as he could break away from whatever it was he did. Her body throbbed; she leaned her hot forehead against the wall, reliving the touch of Warren's skin on hers, his tongue and teeth, nibbling and sucking . . .

The kitchen wall phone rang three inches from her ear, and Frances leaped as though shot.

Without thinking, she answered it.

"Fran? This is Suzy . . ."

Suzy. Suzy—who in hell was Suzy?"

"Jack's secretary?" A small, slightly hurt laugh. "Remember me?"

"Oh," said Frances. "Suzy. Yes, of course— I'm sorry. You scared me."

"I just wanted to check—I mean, I heard you weren't well. Can I help, Fran?"

"Weren't well?" echoed Frances, belligerently, "Who *said* so?"

"Liam called. Listen, if you're sick, I should get a message to Jack—"

"No!" Frances' voice cracked in horror. Jack would come home . . . Warren would . . . she wouldn't be able to see Warren again! "Suzy," she cried, "you listen to me. Liam doesn't know what he's talking about. I'm fine, just fine." (Leave me *alone!*) "Believe me, Suzy, I've never been finer." She hung up, breathless. She took down the cookie jar, feeling upset and disoriented. How dare they disturb her. How dare Liam—She munched, and waited anxiously for the onset of joyful lightheadedness, but nothing happened. Frances wrung her hands together in panic and took another. But it was not until after she had eaten a third, and marched in a frenzy of anxiety up and down the kitchen that the walls began to draw away and the tension drain from her body with the magic. Frances gasped in pleasure. The kitchen cabinets were so yellow, so warm and loving. So radiant. Leaving the coffee pot to perk cheerfully alone on the counter, Frances floated upstairs and spent the morning dreaming of Warren on her mussed bed.

Chetty came home at noon, and so, miraculously, did Connie. "She has short days this week," Frances vaguely remembered Gina saying. "She can take care of Chetty for you as soon as she comes home. It's good for you to rest if you're feeling peaked."

"But Mom," Chetty shouted in exasperation, "I don't *want* to play over at that fat old Connie's house."

"Darling, I'm sorry," said Frances in the throes of a genuine fit of shame, tenderness, and regret. "It's just that Mommy's not well this week, and I have to rest. I'll make it up to you, sweetheart. I promise."

Chetty asked anxiously: "Mom, will you be O.K. by Saturday?"

182

"Sure I will," lied Frances cheerfully.

"It's Halloween," Chetty reminded her. "I'm making my costume at school. It's trick or treat, Mom."

Frances stared at her, dimly remembering how much that meant, how Chetty looked forward to Halloween throughout the year, the time and effort spent on her costume, and the annual kids' party given by Bob and Julie's parents. This year would be a poor substitute, for Frances knew she would never be able to drive into the city, despite the party invitation impaled on the bulletin board in the kitchen. Chetty would be so disappointed, but this year she would have to make the rounds on Woodburn Hills Road and Woodburn Lane. "We *are* going to Bob and Julie's house, Mom, aren't we?" Chetty stared at her anxiously. "You did promise, Mom." Each day, Chetty studied the invitation, trying to read reassurance into the vacuously grinning pumpkin face, and the caption which Liam had told her read: "No Tricks, Just Treats." "I'm going to a party in *San Francisco,* Halloween," Chetty bragged to her friends at school. "I'm going over to Bob and Julie's house. My mom *said* so."

"Are we going to Bob and Julie's? We are, Mom, aren't we?"

Frances ran her fingers through her still unwashed hair and sat up in bed. "Sweetheart, I hope so; I'll try," thinking: Chetty, please go over to the Bombolinis. Please, *please* leave me alone. Her head throbbed, she felt slight dizziness and nausea, and now, an ache between her legs. The last time she had been to the bathroom, as she recalled, it had burned.

183

Chetty's face refused to focus. "I'll try, darling," repeated Frances, unconvincingly.

Chetty shouted with passion: "Mom, if we don't go to Bob and Julie's party I'll hate you. I'll shoot you dead and cut you up into little pieces. I'll hang you up in a tree, and I'll—" Chetty broke into noisy sobs which reached Frances only as a muffled pulsing annoyance of sound. She said: "That's enough, Chetty. I can't stand any more. Please go away."

The child stared at her, small tired face twisted in misery. Dimly Frances thought unsympathetically: "What a ratty-looking kid." Chetty's hair was unbrushed; her dress, which she had worn for four straight days, was stained with food, juice, and paint, as dirty as only a small child's dress could be. Her hands were grimy and her tights torn at the knee. Chetty was a tidy child, who liked to wear nice clothes. She had said in desperation several times: "Please wash something for me, Mom. I don't have anything clean to wear to school." "Of course," said Frances, who had washed nothing, "I'll do it this afternoon." "The kids say I look dirty," Chetty complained tearfully. "They're laughing at me, even." "We'll ask Connie," Frances had said hopefully. "That's it; we'll ask Connie. She'll be glad to do a wash for you." "No!" Chetty had shrieked with violence. "I don't want that Connie *touching* my clothes. I *hate* her."

And now Frances sighed in relief as she heard the sound of sobbing trail away downstairs, heard the voices of Gina and Connie at the front door, Gina's voice shouting heartily up the stairs: "Need anything, Fran? I'm going to take Chetty home and give her lunch."

"She only gives me peanut butter and jelly sandwiches," Chetty had complained. "She never makes me soup. Or scrambled eggs or anything like you do. I don't *want* her lousy peanut butter and jelly sandwiches." Chetty was steadfastly rude to the well-meaning Bombolinis. Amazingly, Frances thought gratefully, they didn't appear to mind. They even seemed to like her. It was incredible.

"Gee, Mom," Connie whined for the hundredth time, "do I have to take that kid to the park again? I *hate* Chetty Driscoll."

(They *don't* like me, Mom. I know they don't. They *hate* me, even—I can tell.)

"Of course you hate her, hon," Gina agreed cheerfully. "But it's just for another coupla days."

Connie's eyes glowed. "I can't wait, Ma. Holy shit, I can't wait."

WEDNESDAY, OCTOBER 28, 2:00 p.m.

Mrs. Van Raalte awoke at last from her drugged sleep of exhaustion. In half an hour she would dress and go down, to eat the one frugal meal a day she permitted herself during her ordeal, but for now she would rest, lie on her back and stare absently at Bill Koeller's face, which for now was flat and dimensionless, merely a photograph. She raised her hands from under the covers, to examine the mottled, loose, old lady skin, the protruding squashy ridges of flesh covering blood vessels

185

and bones, the lumpy knuckles and the ugly nails which would be tinged yellow beneath their heavy coating of lacquer. Hateful, all of it. Hateful face, hateful body, hateful skin, blood and bone; disgusting, every moment of it, this aging, decaying and gradual, inevitable degradation. Three more days until Saturday, October 31. Three more days before she would be free. Mrs. Van Raalte laid one ugly old hand across her chest, which burned sharply for a second or two at the sudden throb of savage excitement which racked her ancient body.

In panic, she clawed for her pills on the night table. Just supposing—

There were just three more days. She had to take care. She must not forget that hers was a heart laboring far longer than its expected tour of duty, must not neglect the routine precautions prescribed by Dr. Spriggs, for by dint of careful rites and detailed preservation, Mrs. Van Raalte had survived one hundred and nine years, eight months and fifteen days. If she survived another three days, she would live forever.

She had been promised.

CHAPTER ELEVEN

Wednesday, October 28, 5:30 P.M.

Liam felt he carried worries enough for the whole world. He had to talk with Florence, but this afternoon, it seemed, twice as many people as usual had flocked to the houseboat with their dumb problems. "It's taking *forever*," he had groaned, pacing up and down the deck. "Don't they *know?*"

But at last even Mr. Dreyfus the artist had wandered dreamily away and Florence sat alone and drained in the comfortable room, hands clasped across her billowing, purple lap, staring vacantly at the empty wall. Finally she asked: "How was she?"

"Stoned again. And looking terrible. She just about threw me out of the house, Flo. She said the doctor was coming. He'd fix her up, she said."

"The doctor?"

"Dr. Spriggs. He's a neighbor. Fran's talked

about him before once or twice. I guess he's O.K. He's got her on vitamin and iron pills."

"Vitamin pills, eh?" said Florence. "And where was Chetty?"

"Next door, with the Bombolinis. That's where the baby-sitter lives—Connie Bombolini."

Florence pursed her mouth. They sat silently beside each other on folding seats, staring in parallel gaze at the wall.

"And tell me about the dog again."

"Grover—" Liam tried to organize his jumbled wits. "Yeah. There's something real odd about Grover. Flo, in the house he crawls about, looking pathetic, like he's sick or something, like I told you. Then, when we get him out, an hour or so later he's frisky as can be. Just fine. Oh Flo," Liam cried, "what the *hell's* going on?"

Florence said: "Believe the cards, Liam."

Liam shrugged. "Flo, it's not that I don't believe the cards. But last night, it was obvious, she was stoned. And again today. And last night, when I tried to see through, all I knew was something was in there she wanted to keep from me. Something she didn't want me to know. I couldn't tell what it was. I thought it must be—I mean, it seemed pretty certain it was—"

"A man," said Florence.

Liam flushed. "That was why I waited, but nobody showed up."

Florence grunted.

"And I—Flo, it *has* to be. Listen, she doesn't want to see me any more. I mean, really. She's just not interested, and that's the truth. It has to mean she's got somebody else—maybe this guy Chetty was talking about, this Warren Pitt. But then nobody came," said Liam.

"Did you ask her if there was someone?"

"No."

"Why not?"

"Flo, knock it off. I suppose I didn't want to know, if you want the truth."

Florence nodded. "It figures."

"That time," Liam cried in anguish, "it meant something to her, the same as me. I *know*. And now, it's like she's completely forgotten everything about it. She hardly knows me any more, and she doesn't even want to see me." Liam glowered fiercely at Florence under his tufted brows. "She's got somebody else. She feels badly about it so she's taking dope. Flo, don't you see? *That's what it has to be.*"

Thoughtfully, Florence reached out her hand to Liam and stroked his wiry head, forcing herself to remember that for all his powers he was still only twenty-two years old and in some areas as inexperienced as a baby.

"You should know better," she said absently, while half-formulated ideas swam around inside her head. If she could only see a pattern.

And then she said, "O.K. Now, listen. Remember what we were talking about earlier?"

"You mean about the—uh—attack thing?"

"Right."

"Yes, but Flo, don't you see—"

"Yes," she said, "I'm beginning to. Now just forget about the drugs, Liam. That's not the point. It's not drugs that have changed Fran."

"Not drugs? But Flo, *surely* that has to be it. Drugs can change anybody's personality. I was hoping—"

189

"You were hoping," she interrupted. "Sure. You wanted some real reason for this mess. Something you could understand, that somebody else could deal with."

"Well, yeah, I—"

"Too bad, Liam," she cut him off again. "Because you may be out of luck. Listen, let's start from the beginning once more."

"O.K."

"Jack and Fran buy this house. Soon after, Fran begins to change some. She drops all her friends. She doesn't start working again. She gets tired and dragged down. Jack goes away unexpectedly. And then—*who* was that?"

"Rosemary Shapiro."

"This Rosemary character calls her, tells her she has to see her right away, and gets totaled. Then what? Fran really goes down. Loses control. Neglects Chetty. Lets the house go. Doesn't take care of the dog. Only sees the neighbors, who she told you already she didn't like. It can't happen so quick, Liam. It makes no sense."

Muttering in her concentration, Florence heaved herself out of the folding chair and headed for the kitchen, her perennial refuge in moments of stress and deep thought. Liam followed.

"Have a cookie," she offered.

"No thanks."

Munching abstractedly, Florence settled her bulk and began to fumble for the Tarot cards; sometimes merely holding them in her hand would help her assemble her thoughts.

"But we don't have to worry so much, surely," Liam said, "if she's seeing a doctor."

"One of the neighbors," snapped Florence.

Liam looked at her. "Flo. Surely you don't think—"

Florence said: "You're one of the only people who can help her, you know."

"And see what happened to me," Liam said bitterly. "I'm no fucking use to anyone."

Florence took another cookie. "A piece of added luck for them, though."

Them.

"Flo, who's *them?* The neighbors?"

"The neighbors," Florence said dreamily. "It has to be the neighbors. There's the Bombolinis, the baby-sitter, the doctor and his wife, and—who else did Fran talk about?"

Liam ran through it once again. "The Spritzers, the Spriggses, a couple of sharp-looking suburban ladies—and Rosemary Shapiro."

"O.K. Forget Rosemary Shapiro. What have we got now?" Florence began to count on her fingers.

"Hey," said Liam suddenly. "Mrs. Van Raalte."

Florence looked at him. "One."

"And the Bombolinis and the kid."

"Four."

"Mr. and Mrs. Spritzer."

"Six."

"The doctor and his wife."

"Eight."

"And the other two women—"

"Ten. And they'll have husbands, won't they?"

"I guess."

"Twelve. There should be one more. There must be someone we haven't counted. Warren Pitt, maybe? Whoever he is?"

There was a pause.

"It's a cone of power," Florence said matter of factly, brushing the cookie crumbs from her chin. "They're after something; there's a purpose. They remove Jack, isolate Fran and kill the one person who might have warned her—who knows why Rosemary Shapiro wanted to warn Fran? Wanted out, maybe? Scared? And the good doctor neighbor is feeding her drugs."

"Flo, that's too *much*."

"Got any better ideas? Listen," said Florence, "It's so simple. She trusts him. He's a *doctor* and doctors are God. We all know that. He gives her these pills—"

"But they're vitamin and iron. Flo, I read the *label*."

"You can say whatever you want on a label," Florence said impatiently. "Don't be so dumb. And he tells her they're vitamins and they'll make her well again. So she takes them without question. Why shouldn't she? God said to do it. Christ, Liam, those pills could be *anything*. And all the time, the neighbors are in and out. The Bombolini kid is taking care of Chetty—"

"And Fran used to say how she couldn't stand Connie. So what are you getting at, Flo? What are we up against, if it's not a drug problem?"

"I'll tell you what we're up against," Florence said, turning to face him, "and you'd better believe it, because you've known all along, inside, I'm right."

Liam said softly: "I suppose."

"It's a coven," Florence said matter-of-factly, "that's what. A whole, fucking, black coven."

Warren Pitt stood in the doorway, smiling down at Frances, the hall light glinting on his golden hair. For the hundredth time, Frances marveled that this could actually happen to her, that she was living this ultimate fantasy, with this beautiful man seeking her out night after night to carry her into far-off lands of sensation from which she prayed each time she might never return.

"You look wonderful," said Warren. Frances laughed self-consciously, pushing at her oily hair. Her eyes glittered and her cheeks were flushed. She had doubled her dosage of vitamins, and she felt marvelous. "Remember," warned Dr. Spriggs, "only at night . . ." She took Warren by the arm, to draw him after her up the stairs. "I couldn't wait," breathed Frances, "I wanted you so much. I didn't know how to get through the day. I didn't know what to do with myself."

Warren grinned, showing perfect teeth. "You didn't?"

She laced her fingers behind his head, dragging his face down to hers. Warren Pitt kissed her, his lips cool against the hectic heat of her eyelids, forehead, cheeks, finally kissing her mouth with savagery, his teeth cutting into her lips. Frances clung to him, pressing her body convulsively the length of his, savoring the moment and postponing with a delicious agony

193

the time of naked struggle upstairs in bed, when their bodies would mingle in the heat and stickiness of shared sweat and juices.

Frances stood in the hallway, head thrown ecstatically back as Warren sucked and gnawed at her throat and ear lobes, feeling with delighted anticipation his jutting rock hardness ground against her belly. "Oh Warren," Frances groaned, "please darling, I must have it. Oh God, Warren, you have to fuck me *now*—please, please, darling, come upstairs—"

She watched him undress, folding his nice clothes carefully and placing them across Jack's bedside chair. His was the most perfect body she had ever seen. She drank him in, from head to toe, the 6-foot 1-inch tanned, supple body, the muscles moving visibly beneath the healthy skin, but not repellently overdeveloped. Not an overstated body, thought Frances with satisfaction. Warren Pitt was an aesthetic compilation of fine, long-fingered hands, powerful shoulders, golden hair, flat, hard stomach, long-boned strong legs, well-shaped high-arched feet. And with fascination Frances' eyes returned to the over-sized male genitals, and the arrogantly up-standing cock which nightly pounded her into aching ecstatic unconsciousness. "Oh Warren," Frances whispered, "I want you so much. I want you *now*, Warren. Please."

Warren stood beside her, where she crouched on the bed, staring up at him, huge-eyed. He said with calm authority: "In a minute, Frances. I want to feel your mouth on me. Suck my balls, Frances."

Frances slipped her arms around his hips, drawing him against her face. She loved to do

194

anything, anything at all for Warren. After several minutes, from far away, she heard his voice again: "Lie down, Frances. On your face. Turn over, and get up on your knees."

"Oh yes, Warren," she murmured gratefully, feeling his long fingers inside her body, and his strong knees pressing her thighs painfully far apart. Frances felt a stretching and a tearing pain, but Warren's right hand was clamped tightly over her mouth as she fell forward under the force of his weight and thrusting power and Chetty never heard her as she screamed.

"But why?" Liam demanded again. "Why are they doing it?"

"Who knows?" Florence put her hands to her head. "It can't be personal. None of them knew Fran before. They have to want her for some reason, and like I said, it can't have anything to do with the house. They could have forced Jack and Fran out of that house without ever lifting a finger; they'd have made sure it was too uncomfortable for them to stay. Jesus, Liam, of all times for you to choose to blank out," said Florence irritably.

Liam looked miserable.

"I shouldn't have said that," Florence said. "I'm sorry. No, there's some reason they must *need* Fran, and if we could only find out—"

"No!" Liam shouted. He clutched at Florence's upper arms. "No—" for suddenly, obediently, the unrelated images in his head began once again to form familiar patterns he could trust. "It's *not* Fran," Liam said, choked.

Florence looked at him sharply. His face was

greenish white, his freckles glaring olive blotches.

"Not Fran," Liam said tightly. "Not Fran at *all*. She's in danger, but only because—It's not Fran they want," Liam whispered, staring at Florence. "It's *Chetty*."

THURSDAY, OCTOBER 29, 2:30 a.m.

"Marta?" said Bill Koeller. "Marta? Where are you?" Awakening properly, he knew with relief that he had been sitting in his chair after all, and not committing indescribable indecencies upon the willing body of Marta Moore on the studio couch. Blinking against the hard, hurting light, noticing the overturned glass, the damp patch on the rug where the ice cubes had melted, the fallen book, the clock which said 2:30 A.M., and the actor and actress in old-fashioned clothes and ugly hair styles who clung to one another on his television screen in a stylized screen kiss, he muttered, "Oh, Jesus, it happened again." He noted then the more subjective changes: the stiffness of his neck and body, for he must have sat locked into one position in his leatherette recliner for hours. He felt the coldness of his apartment (he must have forgotten to turn on the heat) and finally, as he moved cautiously, he felt the cold damp stickiness of his pants. He hurried to the bathroom as fast as his cramped legs could take him, dropped his tacky underwear and examined himself thoroughly, but so far as he could see, everything looked fine. He sat heavily on the toilet seat, stared at his hairy ankles in utmost gloom, and attempted to piece together what had happened to him that night.

There had been a program to watch at eight o'clock; nothing interesting, except for the possibility of seeing one of his own commercials. He had settled with a new spy novel and a Scotch and soda in front of the television set, his ear cocked while he read, waiting for the familiar jingle of the commercial. And then he must have "gone off again," he thought with a sick twist to his stomach, which made it every night since Sunday. Only this time there was something added. He remembered now, with a flush mounting to his ears, the brutal things he had done with an unknown, black-haired rather slatternly woman. Remembered everything. "No," Bill said shrinking, "I'd *never* do anything like that."

On those rare nights when Bill was both randy and dateless, he would find himself after a few drinks curled in bed, holding himself carefully wrapped in the folds of a small towel, enjoying what he had always considered exceptionally lurid fantasies. But these new dreams, illusions, whatever, had to originate from the same source, his own brain, although the things that he did and the man he was in these dreams seemed alien and repellent to him. It would never have occurred to him before, for instance, to whip a woman with a wire coat hanger. Not that he was particularly naive, but his inclinations simply did not lie in that direction. Had some suppressed urges, lurking unsuspected inside him over the years, suddenly exploded to the surface? Could they have been triggered perhaps, by that initial nightmare? Bill doubted it. These were just not *his* ideas. Which could only mean that they were somebody else's. Which meant that another person out there had access to his mind and was directing him in this nightly circus. It was not an attractive thought.

Bill blanched at the very thought of discussing such problems with Dr. Kleinwort, but he knew he must get help soon.

THURSDAY, OCTOBER 29, 2:30 a.m.

It was very late. Neither of them could guess how late it was, but they knew it was long after midnight. All evening they had wrangled, passing one to another, back and forth, the arguments that made no sense, for following Liam's one violent revelation there had been nothing. Part of his mind had lifted, only to close down again immediately, leaving them with no vestige of a clue.

Florence believed him now. The conviction had grown in her all evening that he had to be right, and if so, everything had changed. She sat very still, while the terrible anger rolled around in her head like thunder. For Frances she had felt a detached indignation, but for Chetty—that anyone should dare. . . . Florence knew what could happen in a black witches' ritual, and inside she felt stripped raw, as though her entire body, every cell surface, every fragment, every corpuscle, had become

198

multi-faceted, diamond hard, reflecting a million shafts of barbed, wrathful light. "How dare they think for one second—" began Florence in a dreadful voice. And then, once again matter-of-fact, although Liam could sense the new tension and violently restrained anger, "Well, you're going to have to hustle."

"What do you mean?"

And Florence explained. There were four grand sabbats during the year, held on Candlemas (February 2), Walpurgisnacht (April 30), Lammas (August 1), and Halloween (October 31). These were the festivals at which the powers of the witch reached their highest potency, particularly Walpurgisnacht and Halloween. "What's the date today, Liam?"

"Flo, how should I know? About the twenty-ninth of October: Oh my God!"

"They will be holding a ceremony," said Florence. "There will be something important at stake, something very big. It could be anything—there's no way we can know. They will run through a ritual. To achieve their purpose they will probably raise up a demon, or the Devil himself—"

"Flo, you're not serious."

Florence nodded. "Of course I'm serious."

"But—a *demon?*"

"Demons," said Florence calmly, "do not exist outside of our own heads. But if they think they have one, the effect is the same. They will feel a coldness, perhaps smell decay and rottenness, perhaps even *see* a demon."

"And—Chetty?"

"The demon needs payment for its help. Normally a newborn baby is preferred, but a small child would probably do as well."

Liam gagged. "Jesus, Flo. Listen, can't we call the police? There has to be something we can do—"

Florence laughed shortly. "And what are you going to tell the police? They'd put *you* away. They haven't *done* anything. Not yet . . ."

"Then, what—"

"She'll be safe until Saturday night," Florence said, taking his hand. He clung to her like a lifeline. Her hand was warm and very strong. "Probably until midnight. It's 2:00 A.M. which is the real witching hour; that's when most human cycles have reached their lowest point. So *this* is what you do. Listen."

And Florence outlined her program for Liam, still holding his hand, directing a steady stream of her own energy through this one firm contact into his body. During the next two days there would be no visitors. The following morning, "*This* morning," Florence said, she would hang her black day notice on the door and shoot the bolts against all intrusions from outside. Liam would go nowhere, but stay quietly on the houseboat in peace to marshal his forces.

"But, Flo, I'll have to go over there and see them. Make sure everything's O.K. . ."

"It won't be O.K.," said Florence, "but it'll keep until Saturday. It won't get any worse. There'll be nothing you can do."

"But Chetty. I promised—"

"By tomorrow you'll be able to reach Chetty same as always. *I* promise."

Liam would drink nothing but water, eat as little as possible, and touch no red meat. "Forget your body," Florence commanded. "Take care of it only as you might maintain a machine. That's all it is. It's what's *inside* that counts, right now."

"And on Saturday night?"

"By Saturday night," Florence said "your own power will be back, probably stronger than ever. And remember—they are black witches and their power is negative. Yours is positive and will be their match at any time. All you need is faith. So you get on over there, after dark. And you watch and wait. Their attention will not be on you. When they leave for the ceremony, which you will probably find takes place in Mrs. Van Raalte's house, you will allow them some time to get started, *then* call the police from Fran's house, which will be empty. Report a prowler, a fire, anything. Then hike on over there and get Chetty and Fran out."

"But suppose I'm too late," whispered Liam.

"You won't be too late. You'll be in touch with Chetty all the time."

"But how long do you think it *takes*," Liam asked in an exhausted voice, "to raise a demon?"

SATURDAY, OCTOBER 31, 11:00 a.m.

Bill Koeller sat the other side of the polished mahogany desk from Dr. Kleinwort, who was looking impatient.

The answering service had grumbled: "Doctor's not on call this weekend. We shall have to see Dr. Lieberman. What seems to be the problem?"

"Nothing seems to be the problem," shouted Bill. "I *have* a problem. And Dr. Kleinwort wanted to be *told*. At once!"

"It won't do us any good," said the voice coolly, "if we shout."

But Dr. Kleinwort was contacted, dragged from his Saturday morning tennis game, and sat facing Bill, for whom the blackouts had now assumed secondary importance to the dreams. Last night's had been a shocker. "It's just not me," Bill muttered helplessly. "I don't know what to do."

"Just *dreams?*" demanded Dr. Kleinwort. "So what's wrong? Mr. Koeller, don't you know you're one lucky young man? To have such dreams. My God," the doctor added wistfully, "that *I* should have such dreams." He wrote a prescription for Valium, 10mg.

"The same woman," Bill said, "every night for five or six *hours*, Doctor." And Dr. Kleinwort was interested to note that Bill actually blushed. Repression? Was it possible? Sexual repression in Los Angeles in this day and age? What an anomaly. He should write a paper. Dr. Kleinwort said cautiously, with faint interest: "Anybody you know?"

"No," Bill answered, bewildered. "Nobody. I've never seen her before in my life."

"How strange," Dr. Kleinwort mused. "Would you mind describing the nature of these—er—encounters?"

"Not my style," Bill said hurriedly. "Not at all."

"It depends, doesn't it," Dr. Kleinwort said carefully, "upon what is generally one's style.

If I don't know what happens, I don't know that there's very much—"

"But what I do," Bill protested, "isn't the point. It just isn't *me* doing it, that's the point. I feel out of myself, out of control. It's like I'd been kind of—taken over, if you see what I mean. . . ."

"Oh, dear," sighed Dr. Kleinwort. Here it was again; the possession thing, if he wasn't mistaken. Many of his patients were involved in some aspect of the motion picture industry and the amorphous fringes of show business. They were people whose general grasp on reality was uncertain, and toward them he had developed his own protective policy. Whenever a case strayed out of the purely physical, refer the patient. Quick.

"Oh, dear," said Dr. Kleinwort again. "Taken over, eh?" His eyelids drooped. He began to make small motions of dismissal. He gathered papers, collected his lighter and cigarettes and dropped them into his pocket. He half rose from his seat, his small spark of interest quite quenched. "Oh, come now, Mr. Koeller. There's been altogether too much of this kind of thing lately. It's become absurd. Books, movies—"

"No," Bill cried angrily, "you can't do that. You can't stall like that, tell me it's fantasy, or self-suggestion, or something. This is real. This is *happening* to me. You can't tell me it's just some kind of hysterical symptom. You saw me when I was blacked out. You know what happened. And I haven't told you yet—"

"You mean," said Dr. Kleinwort, "there's more?" He straightened up, his mind more than half on his interrupted tennis game. "Mr.

Koeller, I am an internist. I feel that we should refer your case to somebody better qualified to give it the handling it deserves."

"But, Doctor—"

"Not my department," said Dr. Kleinwort impassively. "Not my kind of thing at all. Now, take one of these every four hours, and if this anxiety of yours continues, call my office Monday morning. We'll set something up for you."

"But—"

"You must excuse me," said Dr. Kleinwort, guiding Bill firmly from the office." I have another appointment. But if you take my advice, get outside a bit more. Play some kind of sport. Tennis, maybe?"

In the lobby, Bill watched the elevator doors close on Dr. Kleinwort, now on his way one level lower to the garage. His last hope, his last link with sanity was gone. He reached in his pocket for the prescription for Valium, and remembered that it was lying on Dr. Kleinwort's desk.

And the office was locked, of course.

SATURDAY, OCTOBER 31, 11:00 a.m.

Liam leaned his elbows on the deck rail. It was high tide, which always made him feel good. Wavelets slapped gently against the sides of the houseboat, and gurgled and sucked between the pilings of the dock. He rested one hip on the rail, breaking up the end of a stale loaf of

French bread to feed the seagull which perched on Florence's roof, head cocked, watching greedily through one glaucous yellow eye. Suddenly he almost reeled into the water, clutching belatedly for support, the bread falling, the seagull swooping after the prize with a rattle of wings and an eldritch screech, as a wave of staggering pain broke inside his head.

The initial blast was followed by successive hammer blows of disappointment and rage. He was unable to think; he could not move. He crouched, eyes closed, on the deck, wrapping his arms around his head, a useless protection against Chetty's formless, battering rage.

Frances, lying exhausted on the bed, noticed nothing immediately, but after several minutes Chetty quieted down and stood with her head cocked to one side as though listening to something. Thank God, thought Frances, gratefully, not knowing that, following the initial soothing burst which spread over her outrage like ointment on a wound, Chetty was receiving a tirade of indignation from Liam.

Chetty's world had fallen about her in ruins. Not only would she not be going into San Francisco to Bob and Julie's party, but her mother had told her that she would be going out trick and treating with Connie Bombolini. "Chetty darling, you know I'd take you myself, but I'm too sick, sweetheart. I'd never be able to go. Please try and understand. It's just for this one time. Next year, Daddy will be home, and we'll all go to Bob and Julie's like before, I promise you."

"I don't believe you," sobbed Chetty. "We're never going again. You promised *this* time! You did. We *never* go anywhere any more. I hate you, Mom! I hate you, I hate you, I hate you!" Chetty's fury gave way to undiluted anguish, and the subsequent wave of energy pounded through Liam like the recoil from a heavy caliber gun.

"If you ever do that to me again," promised Liam, "I'll feed you to the fishes in tiny pieces."

"Sorry, Liam. But we're not going to the party! I'm going out for trick and treat with Connie Bombolini."

"I'll be right over," said Liam.

SATURDAY, OCTOBER 31, 12:00 NOON

Gina Bombolini dialed Mrs. Van Raalte, who was still asleep, a tiny drained figure in the huge, draped bed.

"The hippy brother-in-law's here again," Gina reported, while Connie watched the striped car climb the steep driveway toward the Driscoll house.

"If you bother me once more," snapped Mrs. Van Raalte, "with nonsense like this—"

"But—" Gina quivered with fear, but continued bravely: "Last time he was over, he took the kid out—"

There was a short silence, then Mrs. Van Raalte said, "He mustn't be allowed to do that. Get rid of him."

Gina Bombolini dialed four numbers from memory.

The Spritzers.

The McNaughtons.
The Spriggs.
The Woods.

SATURDAY, OCTOBER 31, 12:05 p.m.

Liam said: "Want to make me a cup of tea or something?"

"O.K.," said Chetty. "If you boil the water. But there's no milk or sugar. I like milk and sugar in my tea. There's nothing—"

"What about you? What about breakfast, stuff like that?"

"I eat breakfast at school, except for weekends. They keep cereal and graham crackers in the office for the kids who don't eat breakfast at home. For the underprivileged kids," Chetty explained seriously.

Liam winced. "And lunch?"

"Mrs. Bombolini gives me lunch."

"Uh huh. That's good." said Liam, and asked suddenly: "Has your mom talked any more about Warren Pitt?"

"Sure," said Chetty. "She's always yelling his name, all night. I hear her. But I don't know who he is. I never saw him. Once I asked her who he was, and she got mad."

"Doesn't he come to visit?"

"No." said Chetty. "Nobody's visited. I guess she's dreaming or something. It's part of her being sick and all, I guess."

"It could be," Liam said, and suddenly began to understand about Warren Pitt. "Hand me

those teabags, Chetty. The water's ready. . ."
He swayed and gripped at the counter with
both hands.

"Uncle Liam?" Chetty asked, concerned. "Is
something wrong?"

Liam took her by the hand. "Yes, Chetty,
there's something wrong. Listen, forget about
the tea. Come on in the living room with me. I
want to talk to you. Quickly." The wave of
blinding nausea had passed, but he recognized
it for what it was and he knew it would return
soon. Upstairs, Frances lay in bed and stared
unseeing into the tree branches.

"So you're not going into the city tonight.
Now, stop it, Chetty. Don't *do* that—" resolutely placing protective barriers between himself and Chetty's indignation. "Now, this is
serious, Chetty—" Liam's voice trailed away,
his lips thinned in his suddenly wan, sweating
face.

"Liam!" cried Chetty. "What is it?"

Liam stood her in front of him and gripped
her small hands in his own. He said hurriedly:
"Now listen. Listen good. I don't have much
time. I'm going to have to get out of here. They
want me out."

"But—"

Liam closed his eyes. "You can see, if you
want, Chetty. Then you'll understand. Be very
very gentle, and for the love of God don't do
anything on your own."

Chetty fastened her eyes on Liam's face,
cautiously let her own mind be caught with his,
and began to cry. "Uncle Liam—you're feeling
sick—and afraid—"

He opened his eyes wide. "Oh yes, I'm
afraid. You're right. And I'll feel just like this

until I get out of here, unless I—unless I turn it around on them. I could do that, you see, but then that would—would let them know who I was. They'd know right away, and I can't risk doing that yet. I still need a little more time." He shook himself. (In her kitchen, Gina Bombolini said: "Surely he should be leaving by *now*. I don't understand . . .") "Now then, Chetty, I'm getting out of here right now, back to Flo. I'll be sending to you all day, so don't worry. But tonight, you've got to be a very brave girl. You and your mom are going to be taken somewhere, and you're not going to like it at *all*." Liam gave Chetty a very brief, doctored flash of the early part of a witches' sabbat. "There'll be black candles, and queer singing, and people dancing around without their clothes on—" ("I *know*," said Chetty, "I *saw*.") "and the *minute* you get there you're to let me know. I'll be at the bottom of the hill and I'll come up right away—" Liam retched. He staggered toward the front door. "And tonight, you and I have got to help your mom because she can't help herself. All around us there are people who are planning on being real mean to her, as well as to you, and we're going to stop them."

"Yes," said Chetty faintly.

"Just call to me," said Liam in a choked voice, "and I'll be right there."

Chetty said: "Please don't be far away, Uncle Liam."

"I won't," promised Liam. "No matter what happens, I'll be right there. Be a brave girl and hang in there. You and I'll fix them. We can fix anybody, right?"

"Right," said Chetty stoutly.

"And I hope to Christ," said Liam as he fell into the driver's seat, "that you'll never have another Halloween like this one."

Chetty stood alone in the driveway, forlornly watching the striped rear end of the Chrysler as it lurched down the driveway. Gina and Connie watched it too.

By the time he reached the freeway and headed south for Sausalito, Liam felt as weak and shaken as though hit by a fierce attack of flu. The intense feelings of nausea and oppression had left him almost by the time he had turned out of the driveway, but he was certain he had been watched all the way down the hill, in case his gradually returning well-being had prompted a return. Nobody, obviously, was intended to visit 40 Woodburn Lane today.

"You were a fool," Florence said later, "going up there. Attracting attention."

"I know," Liam agreed, "but if that's the best they can do—"

"It isn't," Florence warned. "Remember Rosemary Shapiro? Don't take any more chances. Wait until tonight."

"Oh, Flo," said Liam, "I wish you'd come with me."

Florence snorted. "I'd give *anything* to be with you. I'd like to take that old Van Raalte bitch and stuff her with her own broomstick. But if push came to shove, I'd be in the way. You know I'd be in the way. No, Liam, you'll be all right on your own. By tonight you'll have it all back again, and you'll have Chetty with you."

"But Flo, I don't want to have to involve Chetty."

"She's involved anyway. Why not use her as a backup force, if anything goes wrong? If Chetty was able to control that power of hers," Florence said gravely, "there's no one and nothing could stand against her. Like this morning. She crocked you, without even thinking."

"You don't have to tell me."

"And don't forget—nobody knows about her. Or about you either. So get her and Fran out of there, and leave the police to round up the whole fucking bunch. Witchcraft is against the law in Marin County," Florence said sternly. "So is the possession of drugs. And the involvement of minors in this kind of shindig. And just think of the press stories. They'll be crushed," she added happily.

"If you say so," said Liam, "but I'd still feel a lot better if you were there too."

"No." Florence shook her head. "You'll manage easily now."

CHAPTER TWELVE

Saturday Evening, October 31, 6:00 P.M.

"I can't make it tonight. I just got out of the hospital, Blake. I'm all racked up," Bill Koeller said into the telephone. "I have to take it easy."

"Shit, man," said Blake Emerson, whose Halloween parties were legendary, "that's too bad. But listen, if you change your mind, come along over; the action starts swinging around midnight. The witching hour. And I got some real *great* movies, Bill. Far out. You don't want to miss them."

"Some other time, man; don't even talk to me about it." Bill grimaced into the mouthpiece.

"Aah, you fink," said Blake, sounding preoccupied now, planning the last-minute details of his party. "And we got a belly dancer coming. Oh well, so you miss out. Listen, take care. O.K.?"

"Sure," said Bill. "See you." He replaced the

receiver, and studied himself carefully in the mirror. The skin on his face was a hard, glossy red and was beginning to peel. Bill shuddered, poured himself a large Scotch and sat down carefully in his recliner wondering again about the woman. Every night the same woman. Someone he had never met, someone as unsuited to his needs and tastes as was possible. A really sluttish, depraved woman, thought Bill with disapproval. Not my type at all; surely not.

Like most other people in the world, Bill Koeller was a complex mixture. He was generally well-meaning, self-centered, morally apathetic, moderately sensual, lazy, kind so long as it did not involve too much trouble or commitment, essentially honest, with the occasional streak of bad temper and meanness. But now, through this past week, it seemed he was stripped of all those stuffy moderating layers and steadily delaminated, a little more each night, to a hard core of cruel sensuality. And for the first time, coiling in his belly, there twisted an unwilling anticipation for what the night might bring. Bill stared down at himself, at the thick hardening beige whipcord ridge lying fatly across his groin, and touched it gently with his wondering fingertips in surprise.

He shook his head. *Who was she?* Each night the same routine. He would find himself standing outside a large house somewhere in the country—in California? Bill thought so from the accustomed night feel and the familiar smells, but he could never be certain. Lights would show upstairs and in the hallway. He would ring the bell, which would be answered by a tall, black-haired, unkempt woman with distraught face and sunken eyes. They would kiss violently, and he would then take her upstairs, up a deep carpeted stairwell, papered with exotic but tasteful wallpaper, along a passage whose hardwood floor needed sweeping and polishing, past a dozen wilted, smelly plants, into a big bedroom which was messy, cluttered and generally tawdry, although with a good going over it could be an attractive room—even elegant. The rug was pale yellow with a large brown stain (spilled coffee?) in the center. Huge windows opened onto trees, and a black emptiness which Bill assumed in daytime would reveal a wonderful view. There was a big bed with a blue, patterned Mexican spread. He had never seen the bed made up, and the sheets and blanket were sour and soiled. On each side of the bed were small round lamps which cast a gentle benign glow over the fierce endeavors which took place nightly upon it. On the right hung a huge mirror in which, from several positions, Bill was able to watch himself and what he did to this woman, *and it was all so real*, every lurid moment of every carnal act.

Bill would awake early each morning, around 3:30 A.M., sweating, trembling, exhausted and soaked in his own semen, the woman's drowned face imprinted in his mind more clearly than that of Marta Moore. He knew each curve, line and blemish on her face and body, each eyelash, fingernail and pore of her skin, as he had registered every detail of the room. Beside the bed, on the night table which was stained with sticky rings, stood a small medicine bottle. Bill knew she was sick, that something was badly wrong. Well taken care of, he thought she might be beautiful; right now it was hard to see any beauty in that puffy face, wasted, unhealthy-looking body and pallid skin, but such scruples appeared to make no difference to the nightly assaults which she relished as much as, during his madness, he did.

Madness.

Bill wondered: *Am I coming unglued? Is Dr. Kleinwort right? And I'm better off seeing a shrink?*

But if I have to go nuts, suddenly remarked the other, the new and wicked Bill Koeller, *what a way to go!*

Bill started, and stared around the room.

It seemed as though another person had spoken.

At 3:00 P.M. Pacific Standard Time, darkness was falling on the Eastern Seaboard. It unrolled steadily across the country to reach California last, at six o'clock, when the deepening sky tones and black outline of palm trees against bands of plum, indigo, and saffron reminded those few who cared for such things that Los Angeles did, after all, share an approximate latitude with Casablanca, Beirut, and Baghdad.

As the last sliver of the sun's crimson, smog-distended disc dropped below the horizon, hordes of miniature demons, ghosts, witches, skeletons, ballerinas, princesses, Supermen, Batmen-and-Robins streamed as though summoned by a bugle out from their homely front doors into the unknown, clutching paper sacks or swinging plastic pumpkins from wrists, in which to stash the night's tooth-rotting takings. In San Francisco, Bob and Julie, Samantha, Michael, John, and Polly erupted onto Bob and Julie's front steps, giggling in delicious terror in a familiar block now transported magically into an eerie wonderworld of goblins, grinning pumpkins, squeaking hinges, recorded moans, and whistles. "It's scary," cried Polly, the smallest, dragging at Julie's hand. "Trick or Treat!" echoed down the block, rising above the ringing of a dozen doorbells. "Trick or Treat!"

But there were no families in Bill Koeller's block. No small child with a paper sack rang his doorbell. There were no delighted screams, no candy, no draped, bewitched small figures. Bill was left alone and undisturbed to relive his nightmare for the seventh and final time.

SATURDAY, OCTOBER 31, 6:30 p.m.

Thank God, thought Frances gratefully, that Chetty saw some sense. The child had been surprisingly docile all afternoon. At any other time Frances would have been thoroughly disturbed, but now she could only be grateful that for some reason Chetty appeared reconciled to missing Bob and Julie's party and to going out later with Connie to trick or treat down Woodburn Hills Road. For a moment, with knitted brows, Frances attempted to remember what Chetty had been so disappointed about, but their San Francisco friends and their friends' children now seemed so remote and shadowy

216

she could no longer give them faces. There had been a party the year before, Frances remembered with agonized concentration, hadn't there? The kids had had a good time. She and Jack had dressed up—Jack? He had been gone for so long she barely remembered him, let alone their friends. Even Chetty's face was growing indistinct; now that Connie and Gina took care of her so much, unless the child actually stood right in front of her Frances had a hard time remembering even what she looked like.

Nothing was real any more, nothing, of course, but Warren. She lived for the sound of the doorbell from the moment she woke up. She was able to get through the morning with the help of Gina's cookies. Long ago she realized that whatever the mixture Gina used it would not be found in a standard recipe book; also that each day more were needed to achieve the same effect, but so what? Without the cookies she wouldn't survive. Thank God for Gina. Afternoons were difficult, but at six o'clock she took half a dozen or so of the pills, and by eight or eight-thirty, when Warren arrived, she would be floating several feet above the ground.

And then the ecstasy; the six hours or so of intolerable, agonizingly delicious, trance-like insanity which marked their time together; her blank drop into unconsciousness; her lonely waking, and the repetition of the dreadful empty cycle until Warren again rang the doorbell, to delight and humiliate her once more. "Wring me inside out," Frances whispered, a wrenching tremor rippling through her body. Longingly she eyed the medicine bottle. It was only five-thirty, but half an hour shouldn't make any difference, and the pills made her feel so good. And they let her forget some things too: the discomfort when she went to the bathroom, the growing ache in her lower abdomen. As she reached purposefully for the bottle, the telephone rang and Dr. Spriggs said: "How are you feeling, Fran?"

"Not so good, Dr. Spriggs," she answered.

"Gordy."

"Gordy . . . not so great, Gordy."

Dr. Spriggs sounded very cheerful. "That's too bad. Tell you what, Fran. How about doubling up on the dosage of that good stuff of yours."

"I already did."

"You did, huh. Not working so great, is it?"

"No. Not at all, Dr.—Gordy."

"Well then, why not double up again? Make it eight for tonight. Be good to yourself. Walk tall."

"All right," said Frances. "If you say so. It can't hurt, can it? Just being vitamins, I mean."

"No," said Dr. Spriggs happily, "of *course* it can't hurt."

Frances hung up, giggling. Vitamins, indeed. *She* knew better. Holding the bottle in her hand and rattling the contents, she found that there were exactly eight bright little bombs left inside. "Eat me," she chuckled, "and walk tall."

She swallowed all of them, and soon, much faster than usual, her lethargy fell away and she became a real living human being. She could do *anything*—the world belonged to *her*. By seven o'clock she was treading, exalted, among beautiful blue colors, through room after room after room of her loving, warm house.

Chetty followed her warily, all the time sending to Liam. "Mom just took her pills, I guess, and she's acting real odd—keeps walking up and down stairs laughing . . . Connie's just come to take me out trick and treating . . . Liam, I'm scared. I don't *want* to go out."

"Then don't go," he sent back.

"But Mommy says to go. She's pushing me out the door. Her and Connie. She says she wants me with her—and Connie's kind of dragging me, 'cause Mom's walking so fast. She's almost running, Liam. She's acting *real* weird. There isn't *anybody* else with us, it's just Connie and me, but she keeps talking to somebody else, and touching herself all over. Liam! Oh, please come."

"It's starting," said Florence. "You'd better get on over there *now!*"

"Already? But it's so early, Flo. They can't be starting. Not this early."

"I'm telling you," Florence insisted, "they're *starting*. Early or not. Who cares why. So get moving. They need you."

While Bill Koeller's body lay stiffly in the apartment in Los Angeles, Warren Pitt dragged the clothes from a giggling, reeling woman in Mrs. Van Raalte's living room. Bill did not like what Warren was doing, but he could not stop him. And when he tried to speak, the words came out of his mouth all wrong, in Warren Pitt's voice. In every way, Bill was just a spectator, and an invisible one too, for the fifteen other people in the room neither looked at him nor paid him the slightest attention save for the disheveled

219

woman beside him whose name he now learned was Frances, who groveled at his knees, pawing at his cock.

And one and all, from the disgustingly withered yellowish crone with the long fingernails to the pallid thick-lipped boy, they were ugly. Bill had never seen so many ugly people together in one room in his life. The only exception was the child. He hated to see the child. There should never be a child in this room, thought Bill. She had curly blonde hair and huge eyes. She wore a paper grocery sack painted to look like an Indian squaw's outfit—Bill remembered it was Halloween—and a lopsided circlet on her head of paper feathers. She was struggling spiritedly in the arms of a fat teen-aged girl, who snarled: "Keep still, you little shit, or I'll sock you good." The child bit her in the arm. There were yelps and a scuffle, during which the child's grocery sack dress was ripped up the side to reveal a soiled blue tee shirt and white cotton underwear.

The woman, Bill decided, must be the child's mother. She seemed not to care what was happening to her. She was smiling slyly at a short stocky man with hard eyes who was offering her two sugar cubes. She took them, cramming them into her mouth, and Bill cried out to her not to eat them, hearing Warren Pitt's voice, which was his own voice, saying: "Go on, baby—*far out.*" *No*, screamed Bill Koeller soundlessly, *No, please don't.* And Frances looked up at him, the sugar cubes melting on her slightly protruding tongue, her face bleared, looped her arms tightly about his ribs, and slid slowly to her knees and as the other people attended to the still-struggling child, took his cock into her mouth.

Liam gunned the Chrysler out of Waldo Point in a shower of dust and gravel. He roared out of Sausalito towards the freeway, hitting seventy on the on-ramp. He climbed the long rise past Mill Valley and Tiburon, crested the hill and plunged down the curving slope toward Corte Madera and San Rafael. He shot past the shopping center at 80 m.p.h. and the thought flashed through his mind that never, when needed, was the flashing red light of the Highway Patrol behind him.

"Liam! Nobody has anything on! . . . And Mommy's just sitting by herself in the corner. Nobody's talking to her or anything. She's just sitting by herself doing—I don't like what she's doing, Liam. . ." Confusion and a flashing series of fragmented images, then: *"I bit Connie, Liam. She was trying to get me to. . ."* More confusion. Then, *"They've torn off my costume, Liam, and my underwear. I don't have any underwear on, and everybody's looking at me—"*

"Oh Jesus," said Liam, swerving into the Woodburn Hills turn-off with an anguished shriek of rubber. Six more blocks, then turn right, up the hill, past all the neat little ranch houses with the tidy lawns and ivy borders. Only two more miles. *"I'm coming, Chetty,"* cried Liam. *"Hang in there, I'm coming. It'll only be a couple more minutes."* And then the Chrysler's engine sputtered. Liam gazed as though mesmerized at his gas gauge. The needle hovered in the red zone. "Oh Jesus," he said again, "Oh *no*." He pressed his foot to the floor, hoping for some last surge of power to carry him to the top of this first hill, after which momentum might take him a little further. For a second the engine responded, then sputtered again, then died. Liam coasted backwards to park off the road then sat for a moment, his arms crossed over the steering wheel, resting his face on his wrists, crying.

"You ran out of gas? Oh no, Liam. Oh, Liam, how could you do that?"

"Now listen, Chetty, it's O.K. I tell you. I'll think of something—" Liam leaped from his useless car. He glared up and down the dark empty street. There was no traffic, no people, no kids, nothing. Except—one elderly lady opened her front door in the small house across the street. A shaft of yellow light was thrown forward onto the paved path. A small black poodle was thrust out into the front yard, presumably to take its last leak for the day. Liam ran across the street. What luck. He could telephone. He shouted, "Hey, ma'am—ma'am, please, I need some help. Can I *please*—" The woman looked at him in terror. She saw only the wild hair, the dusty Levi's and dirty shirt and outlandish car parked under the acacias. She darted inside her house, dragging the protesting poodle after her, and slammed the door.

Something very interesting was certainly happening. Warren Pitt stretched luxuriantly as the woman worked on him, watching the two men drag the struggling naked child onto the table in the middle of the room. It did not really look like a table. Obviously intended as an altar of some kind, it was covered with a thick black cloth and at each of the four corners flickered a tall, black candle. At the base of each candle was a metal ring, presumably attached to the table, for the child was spread-eagled upon her back and bound to the rings by the wrists and ankles. . . *"Liam, they've tied me to the table! I don't know what they're going to do to me! Liam, I'm so scared. Oh, please, please hurry!"* . . . The room appeared huge to Warren. Any windows were concealed by heavy black draperies. The floor was bare, with two large concentric circles marked upon it with white tape, and in the space between the circles were written a number of words which Warren did not understand although he recognized a few of them for Latin:

In nomina Pa + tris et fi + lii et Spiritus + Sancti! + Hel + Sabaoth + Agia + Tetragrammaton + Agyos . . .

Inside the smaller circle was a five-pointed star.

Headlights, rearing fast behind Liam, threw his long shadow in front of him up the hill and a struggle, fast and urgent, took place in his head. Should he hitch a ride? It was an answer to prayers. Unless it was a latecomer to the sabbat. . . Liam dove into the bushes beside the road and crouched motionless until the twin red tail lights had turned the next corner and vanished.

". . . *Liam,"* gasped Chetty, *"there's this scary old lady; she's looking at me like— like—like she's feeling—"* There was a confusing image which Liam interpreted as covetous anticipation . . . *"and she's standing beside me*

singing. *And all the other people are singing too—kind of weird singing—*" The fear and bewilderment which reached Liam were wrenching. He ran until he thought his heart would burst. *There's this big circle on the floor,*" continued Chetty, trembling, *"with another round circle in it, and inside that there's this kind of star—*" *"A pentacle,*" said Liam soothingly, *"it's called a pentacle.*"

"And I'm on this kind of table, with these lousy black candles round me, Liam, they stink!"

The traditional witch candle, the wax rendered from the bodies of dead murderers, was surely a horror of the remote past, and yet. . . Liam shuddered. Mrs. Van Raalte had a lot of money. And money could buy anything. . . .

"They stink something awful," Chetty was sending. *"And all the people—they're kind of dancing round me, still singing—*" Liam received an abrupt, swooping montage of naked, grotesque bodies and leering faces. How much more terrible they must look to Chetty. . .

"Liam, please, please hurry."

Distorted words reached Frances; words with no meaning—"After all," somebody said, ". . . mother on dope that way . . . take care of a kid . . . no way." Echoing laughter followed. In a panic, she reached blindly for Warren, her only safety in this wild, unrecognizable world, but his strong, beautiful face slipped, blurred, focused again for a second before—melting. Then there was nothing there. "Warren," she whispered, "Warren?" Her voice sounded warped. Her mouth writhed and opened and shut. Her tongue was so dry and swollen that it filled her mouth and now she could not speak at all. Then through a momentary gap in a mass of undulating naked bodies, she suddenly saw an ancient woman so old as to be almost unrecognizable as a human being, holding a large kitchen knife above her head with both hands, its blade glinting red in the flickering lights of the evil-smelling candles. Frances stared at the old woman, at the eye sockets filled with cobwebs and dust, at the dark tips of a spider's legs moving inquiringly at the edges before drawing out the rounded body sac. "Doesn't she know," Frances inquired thickly of the room, "that she's dead and rotting?" And then she began to scream.

The chanting stopped. Nobody paid the slightest attention to Frances. The twelve disciples stood silent and rapt before the altar, inside the inner circle, while Mrs. Van Raalte, in the center of the pentacle, poised the knife above Chetty's body. She raised her eyes, unfocused and fanatic, and in a deeper voice than normal, vibrating with power, began her invocation:

"... Emperor Lucifer, Master of all the rebellious spirits, I beseech thee be favorable to me in the calling which I make upon thy great Minister Ashtoreth, having desire to make a pact with him; I pray thee, also, Prince Beelzebub, to protect me in my undertaking. O Count Ashtoreth! be propitious to me ..."

"Liam," Chetty moaned miserably, *"She's calling to somebody called Ashtoreth—she's telling him to come. Liam! It's getting so cold in here!"*

"Of course it's getting cold," Liam snapped back. *"She's sapping the energy from each and every one of you and drawing it into herself. It's you that's getting cold. Not the room. Listen, I'm almost there . . .*

"Well you'd better hurry up. I don't think she's going to wait much longer."

Frances crouched, still screaming, outside the magic circle, unprotected from the Demon Ashtoreth, the horror of whose arrival would at the very least blast her mind into gibbering wreckage forever. But for now, having no understanding whatever of her circumstances, she was the only member of the company not to feel the intense cold apparently seeping through the room.

". . . And grant me, in exchange for the heart's blood of this child so offered, the gift of eternal life. . . . Oh Ashtoreth, I beseech thee leave thy dwelling in whatever part of the world it may be, to come and speak with me. . ."

Liam stood in front of the massive front door of the Van Raalte house. His heart hammered in his ribs so loudly he feared it could be heard across the county; the blood sang in his ears and his legs trembled. His first impulse was to pound with all his remaining strength on the huge ornate iron door knocker "and scare the shit out of them," he muttered savagely, but then wondered: What would they do then to Frances and Chetty? So he ranged around the side of the house, desperately searching for an unshuttered window. The house could have been deserted; no lights showed at all. Nowhere.

Then, *"Mommy's screaming,"* cried Chetty. *"It's getting awful cold, and now there's this horrible smell coming—like something died— Liam! Liam! LIAM! Quick!"*

Liam found a window at last, around the back, and smashed it in with his elbow. He reached inside for the catch, while Mrs. Van Raalte's carefully installed burglar alarm rang at the Central Answering Service and was relayed instantly to San Rafael Police Headquarters.

Liam crawled through the broken window into what must have once been a servant's washroom. He cut his forearm on a projecting piece of glass, which sliced clear through his denim shirt and deep into the muscle below, but he never noticed, for he could now hear Frances' screams. He let himself out of the bathroom into a passageway floored with polished linoleum, shouldered through a heavy swing door, and padded swiftly down a carpeted corridor, his feet making no sound.

He stood in the high-arched doorway leading into the formal living room, studying the grotesque scene before him, taking quick stock of the situation. The aged crone who must be Mrs. Van Raalte stood with her back to him, half concealing Chetty, who lay bound on the altar. She lay still, struggling no longer, head twisting to look for him, for she knew he must be close. The coven faced toward him, but he was still unnoticed.

"Oh Ashtoreth," repeated Mrs. Van Raalte, "I beseech thee leave thy dwelling. . ."

To his astonishment and dismay, Liam felt

terror strike to his very bones. He stood rooted to the floor, frozen, horribly aware of being outside the protective circle, at the mercy of whatever came to Mrs. Van Raalte's bidding. "Oh, God," he whispered, "Oh God have mercy on me. . ." And Florence's voice spoke to him as clearly as though she stood behind him. *"Demons don't exist,"* she said matter of factly, *"outside of our own heads. . . Don't be a fool, Liam."*

". . . in whatever part of the world it may be, to come and speak with me. . ."

But it was not Ashtoreth who stepped into the living room of the Van Raalte house to answer the summons.

It was Liam.

Mrs. Van Raalte turned very slowly to stare with awful sternness toward the doorway where he stood, her terrible miscalculation, her nemesis in torn shirt and Levi's, the blood beginning to drip from the fingers of his left hand. The rest of the coven, believing him in truth to be a demon in human form, stood for those first vital seconds transfixed with fear.

Liam never dropped his eyes from those of Mrs. Van Raalte. ("There was kind of an electrical noise," Chetty said later. "Like a crackling, sort of, and I could *see* it, too. It wriggled between you and that—that old woman like caterpillars. You know, sort of up and down." "Frequency," Florence said.)

"Frances," Liam said clearly and quietly, "get up and come over here to me."

Mrs. Van Raalte hissed through clenched teeth to her faltering disciples: "Take care of him." And while Liam rocked under the directed malevolence of the entire coven, suddenly doubting his strength, so newly restored, he realized with anguish that he had had no time to call the police.

Florence spoke again. Urgently: *"Chetty, Liam. For God's sake call on Chetty!"*

Liam obediently whispered: *"Chetty, help me."*

There was a searing flash inside his skull, not directed at him but through him, using him as a conductor, powerful in its infinite voltage as a lightning bolt, and Liam knew then beyond doubt, beyond the confused cries, the whimpering of Connie Bombolini, Frances' renewed screams and the agonized shock on the face of Helena Van Raalte, that it was all over.

"Mrs. Van Raalte," Liam said gently, "it's over."

Mrs. Van Raalte's thin gray lips writhed back from her gums in a soundless shriek, her hands clawing toward Liam in a hideous gesture before convulsively clutching at her chest as she slid to the floor.

"Chetty," Liam said in a commanding voice, "don't look."

"Is she dead?" Chetty asked hopefully.

"Yes."

"Good!" she said with satisfaction.

"Then let's go. Come on, Chetty, let's get you off of that goddam table." He picked up the knife from the floor where it had fallen from Mrs. Van Raalte's dying hand, slicing the cords which bound her with four quick strokes. "Will you come *on*, Chetty?"

"But my *costume*," Chetty wailed, grabbing up her Indian outfit from the corner as they ran, and struggling into it. "They tore my costume, and they took my clothes. Liam, I can't go out without my clothes. . ."

"Oh yes you can," shouted Liam. "Now, move it while I get your mother!"

The raging hysterics of Connie Bombolini faded behind them while Liam, with the muttering, sobbing Frances dangling over his shoulder in a clumsy fireman's hoist, pushed Chetty ahead of him down through the tangled brush in the Van Raalte front yard, through the lacerating press of scrub oak bushes, around the grape stake fence, into the temporary haven of the Driscoll driveway. Chetty whined at the assault from the slapping twigs and branches, but plunged forward heroically as a speeding car raced past the foot of the driveway, up Woodburn Lane, followed a moment later by a second, its splintered headlight beams cutting in flashes through the trees.

Chetty clutched at Liam's sleeve. "Someone's after us!"

"No," Liam said after a moment's pause, "that'll be the police."

"Police? But how did they know?"

"I broke a window getting in." Liam shifted Frances' weight more evenly across his shoulders. "It must have rung an alarm. I guess she forgot to switch off her alarm. Maybe she wasn't able to."

"An alarm?"

"A burglar alarm." Then he said sharply "Oh, Christ," as a new thought flashed through his mind: The police would be looking for prowlers; they would search the neighborhood, ring doorbells! "We can't let them find us; not with your mom like this; not looking like this.

230

We've got to get her out of here—to a doctor—"

"Oh, Liam," begged Chetty, "can't we stay?" The house looked so inviting, even in its squalor. The lights still shone brightly from every window, the front door stood ajar, a gleam from the living room window glinting on the polished body of a light-colored car standing in the driveway.

"Who the hell?" asked Liam.

"I know where Mom's car keys are if we've got to go," Chetty said.

"She hasn't driven anywhere for a month," said Liam. "The car won't start, most likely. And anyhow, we can't get out—that car's blocking the garage."

"Oh Liam," Chetty whispered through clattering teeth, dancing a small dance of frustration beside him, "who *is* it?"

Liam stood still for one undecided second, once more hefting the nude body of Frances to a slightly easier position. Each second she weighed heavier, and was now beginning to struggle and beat at his head and shoulders and tear at his face. He heard the distant sound of slamming car doors up at the Van Raalte house, and then Jack's voice, shocking in its anger, shouting from the doorway.

"You son of a bitch," his brother screamed, "what the fuck have you done to Fran?"

Police Officers Murphy and Slovik, in the first area car to respond to a routine Code 2 alarm (Urgent: silent approach), stood in conference on the Van Raalte steps as the second car arrived and disgorged two more men. Sergeant Murphy deployed his troops: two in front, the others to move in back. Then: "Hear that?" said Officer Slovik. "Screams. Oh, boy."

"Inside," cried Sergeant Murphy, making a run for the door.

"It'd take a goddam cannon to break in a door like that," said Officer Slovik, gazing at the massive oak panels.

"No wonder she had a goddam heart attack, carrying on like this at her age." Sergeant Murphy stared down in disgust at the still figure of Helena Van Raalte. "The old bat must be a thousand years old. And will you look at that, for Christ's sake."

Officer Stan Slovik's eyes ranged slowly around the room, the brilliant lights shining down brutally and impartially on the polished wood floor with its magic circles, pentacle and symbols; the smoking black candles; the altar with its metal rings and severed cords. "They musta had someone tied up on that," Slovik said, looking critically down at the knife on the floor.

Alone of the huddling naked figures, confused and still shocked from the aftermath of Chetty's barrage, Gina Bombolini had attempted escape. She had crashed through the front door and lumbered down the steps right into the arms of Sergeant Murphy ("Like a herd of fucking elephants," as he told it later in the squad room). She now sat shouting obscenities in the corner of the room. Connie, having been slapped out of her hysterics, sat mute and shuddering beside her, tears splashing silently onto her fat white legs.

"Thirteen of 'em," said Sergeant Murphy, doing a rapid head count. "That's right for one of them goddam witch deals."

"Sabbat," said Officer Slovik.

"Right," said Sergeant Murphy. "Always knew there was something screwy going on up here."

"Remember that kid last year? The one who tortured the animals?" Officer Slovik jerked his head toward Alan McNaughton. "That's him. I'd remember that little fucker anywhere."

Alan gazed indifferently at them, his colorless eyes enlarged and distorted behind his heavy glasses.

"Christ," said Sergeant Murphy, "I guess we caught ourselves a catch." He looked disgusted. "And what about the other kid?"

"It wasn't me," wailed Connie Bombolini. "I didn't do anything. I don't know anything about it, honest, officer. It was them made me do it. It wasn't me going to kill her—*honest*."

Sergeant Murphy and Stan Slovik looked at one another.

Slovik said: "Better read 'em their rights."

They made an appalling tableau: Chetty, pinch-faced, tear-stained, draggle-haired, clinging to the torn remains of her Indian outfit; Liam gray and drawn, blood in a streak across his face, blood on his arms and hands, blood on Frances' naked legs. Jack looked dumbly at Frances' nude buttocks, at her wildly flailing arms, heard her incoherent cries and drew his own conclusions. He shouted again: "What the fuck have you done to Fran? I'll kill you, you lousy freak!"

Jack attacked Liam with clubbed fists, his intention plain and murderous, but Liam's reactions were still sharp and as yet unclouded by pain and loss of blood, many swift pieces of information flashing across his brain in a fraction of a second. His immediate goal was medical attention for Frances, no matter what. He had been provided miraculously with a functioning car and Marin General Hospital was less than two miles away. Nobody should stop him now, certainly not his enraged brother.

There was nothing else he could do.

Reacting automatically, a machine working beyond thought and emotion, Liam pounded into his brother's mind a fast-driven image of confused terror. Jack cried out once, a sharp bitten-off shout of panic, then stood staring at Liam, swaying on his feet, mouth sagging, his fists dropping helplessly to his sides while the sweat poured down his face.

"Get in the back," snapped Liam, while Jack struggled for breath. "Sit down in the back and take care of Fran." And Liam bundled the bulk of Frances in after him, now dangerously quiet and comatose.

He never remembered the drive to the hospital. The final thrust at Jack had drained him, and by the time he reached the bottom of the hill and swung right onto Sir Francis Drake Boulevard, he felt very cold, very tired, his hands and feet responding sluggishly to the commands of his brain. It was still quite early on a Saturday evening, and traffic was heavy. With his brother passive in the back seat, Frances in shock and Chetty terrified and squalling beside him, Liam batted the rented sedan between swooping headlights, blaring horns and the tearing screeches of rubber on pavement, avoiding an accident with what could only have been sublime intervention. He rocked into the left-turn lane, lurched through the intersection against a red light passing across two approaching cars with a split second to spare. On down a steep grade, weaving through a narrow stretch of road construction, ploughing through conical red road dividers and knocking aside temporarily erected barriers and road signs—"Caution," "Men at Work"—while the oncoming cars scattered to either side of him like quail. Mercifully, after several decades, he saw the huge white sign ahead and above him with the blue lettering: EMERGENCY, with an arrow pointing sharp left.

Liam took the corner at forty miles per hour, his foot resting like a slab of immovable lead on the gas pedal, roaring up the final stretch of roadway, seeing white and yellow lights swinging toward him impossibly fast; hearing shouts; seeing running figures. . . With a final effort, Liam dragged his foot from the gas pedal and hit the brake. The tormented car bucked and stalled, coming to rest inches behind a parked ambulance, and he fell forward onto the steering wheel, into a dark, endlessly echoing pit, where a horn somewhere blatted on and on and on . . .

While Sergeant Murphy had, as he put it, "controlled the situation," called the coronor's office, demanded the assistance of trained investigators, arranged for the dispatch of Connie Bombolini and Alan McNaughton to Juvenile Hall, and examined the goodly array of amphetamines, hallucinogens, and, as Officer Williams said, "enough pure heroin to OD an elephant"; while Liam and Frances Driscoll were speeded into the Emergency Room at Marin General Hospital, Jack stood blinking and stretching aching jaw muscles and Chetty danced, wildly nervous and overexcited in her torn paper costume; while Florence Rossi paced up and down the length of her houseboat, hands clasped in front of her and enormous, fat tears streaking down her face, Bill Koeller woke stiffly in his chair, looked at his watch, and noted that it was only 9:00 P.M. So early for it to finish? Could this be the end? It *was* the end; somehow he knew beyond doubt that it was definitely all over, and he was free. But it had been one doozy of a week, when he had exultantly savaged away his nights as Warren Pitt. . . . Man, that had been *living!*

Warren Pitt. It wasn't such a bad name, thought Bill. In fact, not a bad name at all. He had this strange feeling that he might be more successful as Warren Pitt. In fact, *pretty* goddam successful. And Bill Koeller was really a *nothing* kind of name, if you thought about it. Warren Pitt had *class*. . . . He decided to call Morrie on Monday, and arrange to work under his new name, and then, studying his face closely in the mirror, wondered whether, with his fading sideburns cunningly concealed with makeup, he might not still go to Blake's party. The lights would be dim enough. It was only nine o'clock, and he had learned a lot this past week.

He picked up the telephone.

"Marta," Warren Pitt said with a smile that was somehow unpleasant, "what are you doing tonight?"

Jack sat wearily in the office of the Emergency Room, around him the noise and bustle concurrent with another action-filled Saturday night—and Halloween, at that. He said, exhaustedly testy, "No, I don't goddam know what happened. It must have been an accident; I wasn't there. I just got out of a goddam plane. . . Why don't *you* tell me what's happened to her, why she's out cold, why she's all bloody. . ."

And no one to meet him at the airport; Liam of course unavailable; the phone call to his bewildered parents ("But Jack, Margie *talked* with Fran and said she sounded fine"); the familiar hassle with his luggage, which was lost; the renting of a car, and the unnerving drive through San Francisco, so tired and worried, into the Marin Hills, to a deserted house blazing with light, whose front door stood open, where he found Frances' purse lying on the floor and his own Western Union telegram unopened on the coffee table. And the house filthy and stinking; garbage on the floor; dirty dishes all over the kitchen; the puppy, frenziedly welcoming, unfed, unwatered, uncleaned up after. His apologetic secretary had guessed right: something *was* wrong with Frances. But where the hell was she? Where was Chetty? Jack's head swam with exhaustion. He had spent the past twenty-four hours in airplanes, missing connections, waiting at airports (at Kennedy, all airport personnel were on strike and he was not even able to buy a drink), and now nobody was here, not a goddam soul—no wife, no daughter. Jack crossed to the phone to call the police, which was when he heard noises outside, heavy dragging footsteps, and a small tearful voice, unmistakably Chetty's, saying: "I know where Mom's car keys are. . ."

And there stood his brother, of whom old

suspicions were instantly aroused, holding Frances over his shoulder, an obscenely naked Frances kicking with bloody legs, who mumbled and shouted in an unnerving gabble, and Chetty, who must have been witness to God knows what nameless depravations, standing beside Liam, tired-looking, dirty and crying . . .

Still dazed, holding Chetty by the hand, Jack had followed the two stretchers bearing the inert forms of Frances and Liam into Emergency, trembling now in the reaction following Liam's mental assault.

"No," he cried in confusion to the nurse sitting opposite him, "I don't have one goddam *idea* what happened. I don't know if they'd been driving. Jesus, woman, I only got in an hour ago from Saudi Arabia—be quiet, Chetty."

"But I want to *tell* you, Daddy."

"Your wife's full name?"

"Frances. . ."

"Last name?"

"Uh—Driscoll. Goddam it, Driscoll. Frances Mary Driscoll."

"Address?"

"What are they going to do with her in there? Where'd they take her?"

"A thorough examination, Mr. Driscoll."

"Listen, I have to *see* her. Where's the *doctor*?"

"Mr. Driscoll, I have to get the information for her record. Which company are you insured with?"

"Goddam it," shouted Jack, "how do I know? You tell me. Take my whole goddam wallet!"

"Daddy!"

238

"Mr. Driscoll! Please control yourself . . .
Doctor!"

Dr. Ciaccone was small and dark and looked
about eighteen. His manner however wás
soothingly professional. "We have to have a
history, Mr. Driscoll, before we can do anything. Otherwise we can't know where to begin. You understand, it's for the good of your
wife." And the endless questions.

"How long has she been unconscious?"

"About ten—five to ten minutes. I'm not
sure."

"And how did you find her?"

Something exploded in Jack's head. Naked
and bloody in my brother's arms, he wanted to
shout. But Chetty was there. He said: "You'll
have to ask my brother about that. She was
with him."

"Please," said Chetty, "Uncle Liam was hurt
awful bad. Is—will he—be all right?"

"Your Uncle Liam will be just fine," said Dr.
Ciaccone. "They're fixing him up right now.
They're going to clean him up, sew him up real
good and put a nice big bandage on. You'll see
him tomorrow, and maybe he can go home
Monday."

At Dr. Ciaccone's request, a hospital volun-
teer took Chetty to the cafeteria for supper.
And the questions went on:

"Is your wife normally healthy? Is she under
a doctor's care? Is she on any medication? Is
she allergic? Does she drink? What drugs
has she been taking?" And, "I want to do some
tests on your wife, Mr. Driscoll. I'll need your
signature here. . ."

239

Dr. Ciaccone said: "The blood wasn't your wife's, Mr. Driscoll. Your brother was bleeding heavily all over her."

"That's something," said Jack, and demanded: "But why do you need a spinal tap? And a pelvic examination?"

"It's possible your wife has been raped, Mr. Driscoll. I'm sorry. There'll have to be a—"

"Oh Jesus God," said Jack, "where is he? I'll kill him—"

"Mr. Driscoll, now take it easy. I only said it's possible."

"The son of a bitch. Where did you put him?"

But Liam lay safely and softly floating in a far-off white world of his own down the passage, lapped in a wooly sea of Demarol, free of responsibility, content for his body to be manipulated and moved around like a loose-limbed doll, while Frances was propped, sagging, for a chest X-ray, catheterized, a needle taped to the inside of her wrist for an intravenous drip. The vaginal smear had been negative for semen.

Jack was allowed one brief look at Frances, all tubes and swinging bottles, before she was wheeled away.

"Try not to worry, Mr. Driscoll," said Dr. Ciaccone. "We're doing all we can. We'll just have to wait."

By midnight, Frances was stabilized enough to be moved into a private room, where she called, between periods of exhausted dozing, for Warren Pitt. At 8:00 A.M., alternately torn between wild excitement and tremulous depression, she remembered Liam.

Jack Driscoll slept from one A.M. onward, heavily sedated.

"Liam," said Frances, weakly insistent. "I've got to talk with Liam. Please. I have to talk with Liam."

He was pale and subdued, his arm heavily bandaged, when they brought him in.

Frances plucked at the sleeve of his good arm. "Liam, please. What happened? Why am I here? Where's Warren, Liam? What happened to Warren?"

"Oh Jesus," said Liam.

"What happened to him, Liam. Oh, please, is he all right? I remember being in that room. There were a lot of people there. You were there too, weren't you? And he was there and then—then—" Frances' eyes opened wide in horror. "I remember—Liam! Warren just—went away, and there was an old lady with spiders crawling out of her eyes—" Frances flung herself against the pillows and her mouth opened in a soundless scream.

"Hush Fran. Hush now. Calm down—" Liam grasped at her agitated hands.

"*Warren*, Liam. *What happened to Warren?*" Frances beat at the bedclothes, and the tubes and bottles rattled and swung.

"You'll have to leave now, Mr. Driscoll." The nurse materialized at his side.

"I want Warren! Please!"

"Hey, listen, Fran," Liam patted her shoulder gently. "Warren's O.K. Now you just go to sleep and we'll talk later."

"You must listen to me, Fran. I know it's hard—" Liam, almost restored, mentally

241

reached into Frances' disordered brain with calming gentle fingers.

"Liam, don't play around with me. Where's Warren? I know something happened. Something's wrong—"

"There's no Warren, Fran."

"What d'you mean?"

"What I'm telling you. There is not and never has been any Warren."

"You're crazy!"

"No, Fran. I'm sorry."

"Liam, you *are* crazy. Listen, I tell you, I saw him every night. He'd come every night, and then we'd—and, he was there in that room. I *saw* him—"

"There was no Warren. You have to believe me."

"But how *can* I believe you? Liam, you're being cruel. You can't say these things to me. Warren is the most real thing in the world. These past weeks he's been the *only* real person—with any meaning—"

"Fran, I do believe you. I know Warren seemed—"

"Warren did not *seem*. Warren was. *Is*. I'm telling you, Liam, I know he was there in that room." The tears rolled unheeded down her wasted cheeks. "For Christ's sake, Liam, do you want me to spell it out for you? I was sucking his—"

"No, Fran." Liam took both her hands in his, trying to still the trembling, the wild tossing of her head, the anguish and horror. He had to. Before Jack saw her. And he had so little time. "Now, listen, Fran. Easy. You were drugged. You've been drugged for weeks. I don't know how they got it in you but they did.

242

Probably those pills Dr. Spriggs gave you. And that wasn't all. Fran, honest, you've got to *believe* me. You've been half out of your head all the time."

"But I *know* that Warren and I—" Frances raised desperate eyes to Liam, and the words rolled out, heedless and uncaring. "You see, inside, I'm all torn—they thought I'd been raped—and I've got an infection—and it hurts, Liam. I *know* that Warren and I—I mean, how *else*, for God's sake, would I?"

Liam said nothing.

Frances recoiled, her eyes widening. "Liam—Oh, God. Liam, if you say there wasn't—if you're right and Warren didn't—"

He stroked her hand.

"Then it must have been—" she could not bring herself to say it.

"It must have been you," Liam finished for her.

"Oh no," Frances trembled, "Oh, no; please, Liam, no. But it *hurts*."

"It was you," said Liam, "but it wasn't you. Try and understand. You've been living in a fantasy world all this time, and now you've woken up, that's all. Warren's gone. Warren went when Mrs. Van Raalte stopped projecting him to you. Think of it as that, as a thought projection, a kind of hypnosis."

"Liam—" Frances grasped at his wrist with surprising strength. "You have to have them bring me something so I can sleep. I can't face it. I can't bear all this now."

"I'll try," said Liam, "but I wouldn't count on it. I don't suppose they'll let you have even an aspirin right now, but I'll try. Now listen,

Fran, you've got to get yourself together. Jack's here—"

"*Jack?* Oh Liam, no. I can't see Jack. Not now." Frances twisted the sheet between her fingers. "But how did Jack—I mean, he's not supposed to be here until next week."

"I told the office you were sick, and they sent a cable. Chetty's over with Kevin and Marge, so she's O.K."

"Chetty! Oh God," whispered Frances. "And she's O.K.? Oh, Thank God. I'd forgotten—Oh, Liam, I'd forgotten about Chetty!"

MONDAY, NOVEMBER 2, 11:00 a.m.

Jack looked at his younger brother with a cold rage. "So will you tell me what else makes any sense? I always knew there was something wrong with you, you dirty—"

"Just wait," Liam interrupted wearily. "It's all getting cleared up."

"I don't have to wait," Jack snapped. "I know what you've been thinking about Fran all these years. Jesus Christ knows what you did to her, or made her do, with all those fucking drugs."

"Oh, knock if off, Jack." Liam said, his head drooping, knowing again the utter futility of trying to communicate with his brother, regressing once more to a sulky child confronted with an angry, uncomprehending adult. But this time a small shaft of hope sparkled brightly a long way ahead as he remembered that in extremity he had torn away all the bar-

244

riers and had, against belief, reached Jack's mind. No matter that the confrontation had been a brutal one; there *was* hope. Someday . . . "Don't yell at me," begged Liam, "until you've heard everything. Please."

"You sit there and tell me Fran was abusing *herself,* and then expect me not to yell at you? That's filthy, man. Fran would never *think* of—"

"But it wasn't a question of what Fran thought," said Liam. "Never."

"She's covering up for you," said Jack. (*"Please, Jack, listen to me. Liam never touched me. Nobody raped me. Please, you've got to believe me—"*) "Anyhow, soon as she's out of here, I'm taking her back to an apartment in the city, so I'll be right there. And so help me, she's never going to see you again in her life."

"She *should* go back to the city," Liam agreed tactlessly. "It's much safer there."

Jack glared at him.

They sat on a bench in the hospital lobby, a yard of space between them, Liam discharged now, to return in five days for the removal of his stitches. Upstairs, Frances' mind still ranged hysterically in her embattled body, but she would recover. After a while.

Jack said brutally: "And *I* don't want to see you again, either. You can just get out of my life, like I never had a brother."

For a moment their eyes held, Jack's blue and hard, Liam's tawny and distressed, hearing the bitter words and knowing that Jack would regret them very soon, but unable to defend himself against the hurt of *now*; knowing also that although a time would come when he

245

and Jack might reach one another, it was not yet.

"I'll be going, then," said Liam. "They know where to reach me."

Jack grunted, and stared down at his locked hands. Then, with a sudden pang—*was* Liam telling him the truth, about all those crazy witches and all? "Oh shit," he said, "I'll give you a ride to Sausalito."

"That's O.K.," said Liam, stiffly dignified, "I'll manage."

"Come on, man. How else are you going to get there?"

"I'll hitch."

"No way. Not with a bad arm." It was suddenly important to get Liam to Sausalito.

"I'll be fine," said Liam, but conceded: "You could take me to the freeway, if you want. I'll easily get a ride from there. You ought to be staying here for—for Fran."

"Well," said Jack, "if you think you'll be O.K. Anyhow, there's always Florence. She'll take care of you."

"Yes," Liam said absently, "there's always Flo."

They left the hospital together into the warm blue morning, and Jack dropped Liam off on a strip of grass a hundred yards or so before the freeway on-ramp, a slender figure standing facing the traffic, the sharp sunlight glinting on his red hair, bandaged arm held stiffly in front of him under the patched blue denim shirt, waiting for his ride to Sausalito.

Jack swung the Camaro in a steep, illegal U-turn, involuntarily searching, on his way back, for a quick glimpse of his brother.

But Liam was already gone.